A Collection
of Short Stories

Nikolai V. Gogol

CONTENTS

- A May Evening
- Old-Fashioned Farmers
- The Calash
- The Mysterious Portrait

A May Evening

As it appeared in the May 1887 Cosmopolitan journal

THERE were sounds of merriment in the village, and a chorus of song murmured, stream-like, through its single street. It was the hour when lads and lasses, after their hard day's work, meet in the mellow gloaming to express their feelings in melodies which, though glad, are never without a strain of sadness. The pensive eventide was dreamily embracing the blue heaven, and transforming every visible object into something vague, shadowy, and ghost-like. The brooding gloom settled into night, and still the stream of song flowed on without surcease.

Guitar in hand, the eldest son of the village headman steals away from his comrades, and makes toward a house that is half hidden by a screen of pink-blossomed cherry-trees. As he walks, the young Cossack strikes a few notes on the instrument, and steps a measure to his own music. When he reaches the house, he stops, and, after a short pause, touches his guitar again, and sings a song of love, soft and low:

> "The sun is low, the night is near,
> Come, oh, come to me, sweetheart, dear!"

"No use," murmured the Cossack when he had finished his song, at the same time drawing near to the window. "My darling is asleep. Hahn! Hahn! A pet diminutive for Hanna are you asleep, or don't you like to expose your pretty face to the cold? Or maybe you won't come out for fear we may be seen together. But there is nothing to fear. The night is warm, and there is nobody near. And if anybody does come, I will hide you in my arms, and none shall see you. And if the wind blows cold, I will press you to my heart, warm you with kisses, and put my cap on your tiny feet, my darling. Only look out for one moment: put your hand out of the window that I may touch your rosy fingers.

"No, you're not asleep!" he adds, passionately, after waiting in vain for an answer. "You are laughing at me. Well, laugh if it pleases you. Good-bye!"

He turns round, throws back his cap, and, still gently touching his guitar, draws a few paces away. Almost at the same moment the wooden handle of the door begins to stir, the door opens with a squeak, and a girl in the spring of seventeen appears on the threshold, and, still holding the handle, she looks furtively around. Her eyes shine in the dusk like little stars, and even the pink flush on her cheeks is not unobserved by the young Cossack.

"How impatient you are!" she whispers. "You were actually getting angry! Why did you come when there were so many people about? I am all of a tremble."

"Never mind, my darling; come closer to me," replied the lover, laying aside his guitar, and sitting down on the door-step. "You know that to be one hour without seeing you is a great trial for me."

"Do you know what I am thinking?" interrupts the girl, looking at him pensively. "I am thinking — something tells me that in the future we shall not be able to see each other so often. I don't think the people hereabouts are good people. The lasses look jealous; and as for the young men — My mother, too, she has begun to watch me more of late. I own I was happier amongst strangers before I came here." And a shade of sadness settled for a moment on her beautiful face.

"Only two short months in your native village, and you are already unhappy! Perhaps you are getting tired of it and — of me?"

"Oh, no; I am not tired of you," she answers, with a smile. "I love you, you dark-browed Cossack! I love you for your hazel eyes; and when they look into mine, my soul answers back, and I feel happy and glad. And I like to hear you play on your guitar, and see you walk about the street. Oh, I like it so much!"

"My own Hahn!" exclaims the Cossack, in an ecstasy, kissing the girl and drawing her closer to him.

2

"Wait, Leoko! That is enough. Now, tell me, did you speak to my father?"

"Wha-at!" he asks, as if suddenly waking from a dream. "Speak to your father! Yes, I said that I wanted to marry — to have you for my wife. Yes, I spoke to him."

The words "I spoke" seemed to fall from his lips reluctantly and almost sadly.

"Well?"

"What can you make of him? The old curmudgeon pretends to be deaf. He won't hear, and keeps scolding because I go about with the boys. But don't think about it, Hahn. On the word of a Cossack, I'll bend him to my will before I've done."

"You have only to say a word, Leoko. It shall be as you wish. I know that by myself. At any other time I should not have listened. Now, in spite of myself, I could not help doing whatever you ask me."

"Look! look!" she went on, resting her head on his shoulder and raising her eyes to the warm sky. "Look there! Far, far away are glimmering little stars: one, two, three, four, five. Is it not true that those are angels, opening the windows of their bright little homes, and looking down on us? Is it not so, my Leoko? Are they not looking on our earth? What if men had wings, and could fly up there! Yet, not one of our trees reaches the heavens. Still, people say there is a land where grows a tree whose topmost branches touch the sky, and that, on Ascension Day, God comes down by it to earth."

"No, Hahn! God has a ladder which stretches from Heaven to earth. On Ascension Day holy angels let down this ladder, and, as soon as God puts his foot on the first rung, all evil spirits take to flight and fall headlong into hell. That is why, on the Lord's Day, there are no evil spirits on earth."

"How gently stirs the water — just like a babe in a cradle!" says Hanna, pointing to a pool hard by, begirt with weeping willows, whose melancholy branches drooped in the water.

On a hillock near a pine wood, slumbered an old wooden house, with closed shutters; the roof was covered with moss and weeds, the windows were half hidden with apple-trees, the dark pines veiled it with shadows and gave it a weird and specter-like look.

"I remember as though it were a dream," went on Hanna, keeping her eyes on Leoko, "that long, long ago, when I was very, very little and lived with mother, I used to hear terrible stories about that house. I am sure, Leoko, you know all about it."

"God be with it, my darling! Don't mind what old women and fools say. You would only be frightened and would not sleep if I told you."

"Oh, no; go on and tell me, like a dear good boy!" she said, throwing her arms round his neck, and pressing her cheek to his. "You don't love me; I know you don't: you only pretend. You have another sweetheart; I am sure you have. You must tell me about the old house. I shall not be afraid, and I shall sleep all the same. But if you don't tell me, I shall not sleep a bit; I shall be thinking, thinking all the night through. Do tell me, Leoko!"

"I shall think soon that what people say is true: every woman is possessed by her own peculiar devil of curiosity. Well, listen. Long, long ago there lived in that house an old man, who had an only daughter. She was handsome; her face was as white as snow — just like yours. Her father was a widower, on the look-out for a second wife. 'Will you continue to love me as you do now when you marry again, father?' she would ask him. And then he would say: 'I shall, my daughter; I shall love you more ardently than ever, and go on giving you earrings and ornaments as I have always done.'

"The old man married and brought home his young wife. She was a fine woman, that wife of his, with a blooming red-and-white complexion and big black eyes; but she cast such an evil glance at her step-daughter that the girl shrieked in deadly fear, but not a word did the step-mother speak to her all day long. When night came and the father and his wife retired, the girl locked herself up in her own room, and, feeling sad, bent her head and fell a-weeping. A little while after, happening to look around, she spied a fierce-looking black cat creeping toward her. Its fur was all a-flame, and its claws struck on the floor like iron. In her terror the girl jumped on a chair;

4

the cat followed her. She sprang into bed; the cat sprang after her, and, flying at her throat, began to choke her. Tearing the creature away, with a cry she flung it on the ground; but the next moment it was again crawling toward her, its savage eyes burning with rage. Rendered desperate by terror, the girl seized her father's sword, which hung on the wall, and with a single stroke cut off the cat's left paw; whereupon the cat immediately disappeared.

"All the following day and the day after, the young wife kept her room. When she came out on the third day, her left hand was bandaged, and she carried the arm in a sling. Then the poor girl knew that her mother was a witch, and that she had cut off her hand. On the fourth day the old man ordered his daughter to hew wood, draw water, and scrub the floors, as if she was a menial servant or a common peasant. On the fifth he chased her from the house, without giving her either shoes for her feet or bread of money for a journey. The poor girl could bear it no longer, and, covering her face with her hands, she wept bitter tears.

"'You have ruined your daughter, my father!' she cried. 'The witch has cast her spell over you, and wrecked your soul. May God forgive you! As for me, He has not willed that I should remain much longer in the world.'

"And look!" went on Leoko, pointing toward the house. "Do you see that high bank? Well, from that bank she threw herself into the pool, and since then she belongs no more to the world. That, Hahn, is what the old folks say; but they say so many things! The present owner wants to sell the house, and they talk about turning it into a brewery. But I think I hear voices. The lads and lasses are coming home. Good night, darling; don't think about that old woman's tale. I dare say it is all nonsense."

And then, after embracing and kissing her, he went away.

"Good night, Leoko!" answered Hanna, whose gaze was still fixed on the dark pine wood.

As she looked, a great fiery ball rose slowly from the shadows, and seemed to fill the earth with a triumphant splendor. The pool was lighted up with a shower of sparks, and the pine wood on the hill began to stand out from the background of dark green.

When the merrymakers had passed, and their voices had died in the distance, every sound was hushed, night covered the earth with a mantle of silence, and Hanna, after a last, wistful glance in the direction taken by her lover, drew back into the house, and closed and bolted the door.

Old-Fashioned Farmers

I am very fond of the modest life of those isolated owners of distant villages, which are usually called "old-fashioned" in Little Russia [the Ukraine], and which, like ruinous and picturesque houses, are beautiful through their simplicity and complete contrast to a new, regular building, whose walls the rain has never yet washed, whose roof is not yet covered with mould, and whose porch, undeprived of its stucco, does not yet show its red bricks. I love sometimes to enter for a moment the sphere of this unusually isolated life, where no wish flies beyond the palings surrounding the little yard, beyond the hedge of the garden filled with apples and plums, beyond the izbás [cottages] of the village surrounding it, having on one side, shaded by willows, elder-bushes and pear-trees. The life of the modest owners is so quiet, so quiet, that you forget yourself for a moment, and think that the passions, wishes, and the uneasy offspring of the Evil One, which keep the world in an uproar, do not exist at all, and that you have only beheld them in some brilliant, dazzling vision.

I can see now the low-roofed little house, with its veranda of slender, blackened tree-trunks, surrounding it on all sides, so that, in case of a thunder or hail storm, the window-shutters could be shut without your getting wet; behind it, fragrant wild-cherry trees, whole rows of dwarf fruit-trees, overtopped by crimson cherries and a purple sea of plums, covered with a lead-colored bloom, luxuriant maples, under the shade of which rugs were spread for repose; in front of the house the spacious yard, with short, fresh grass, through which paths had been trodden from the store-houses to the kitchen, from the kitchen to the apartments of the family; a long-legged goose drinking water, with her young goslings, soft as down; the picket-fence hung with bunches of dried pears and apples, and rugs put out to air; a cart full of melons standing near the store-house; the oxen unyoked, and lying lazily beside it.

All this has for me an indescribable charm, perhaps because I no longer see it, and because anything from which we are separated is pleasing to us. However that may be, from the moment that my brichka [trap] drove up to the porch of this little house, my soul entered into a wonderfully pleasant and peaceful state: the horses trotted merrily up to the porch; the coachman climbed very quietly down from the seat, and filled his pipe, as though he had arrived at his own house; the very bark which the phlegmatic dogs set up was soothing to my ears.

But more than all else, the owners of this isolated nook—an old man and old woman—hastening anxiously out to meet me, pleased me. Their faces present themselves to me even now, sometimes, in the crowd and commotion, amid fashionable dress-suits; and then suddenly a half-dreaming state overpowers me, and the past flits before me. On their countenances are always depicted such goodness, such cheerfulness, and purity of heart, that you involuntarily renounce, if only for a brief space of time, all bold conceptions, and imperceptibly enter with all your feeling into this lowly bucolic life.

To this day I cannot forget two old people of the last century, who are, alas! no more; but my heart is still full of pity, and my feelings are strangely moved when I fancy myself driving up sometimes to their former dwelling, now deserted, and see the cluster of decaying cottages, the weedy pond, and where the little house used to stand, an overgrown pit, and nothing more. It is melancholy. But let us return to our story.

Afanasii Ivanovich Tovstogub, and his wife Pulcheria Ivanovna Tovstogubikha, according to the neighboring muzhiks' [peasants'] way of putting it, were the old people whom I began to tell about. If I were a painter, and wished the represent Philemon and Baucis on canvas I could have found no better models than they. Afanasii Ivanovich was sixty years old, Pulcheria Ivanovna was fifty-five. Afanasii Ivanovich was tall, always wore a sheepskin jacket covered with camel's hair, sat all doubled up, and was almost always smiling, whether he was telling a story or only listening. Pulcheria Ivanovna was rather serious, and hardly ever laughed; but her face and eyes expressed so much goodness, so much readiness to treat you to all the best they owned, that you would probably have found a smile too repellingly sweet for her kind face.

The delicate wrinkles were so agreeably disposed upon their countenances, that an artist would certainly have approplife, led by the old patriotic, simple-hearted, and, at the same time, wealthy families, which always offer a contrast to those baser Little Russians, who work up from tar-burners and pedlers, throng the courtrooms like grasshoppers, squeeze the last kopek from their fellow-countrymen, crowd Petersburg with scandal- mongers, finally acquire a capital, and triumphantly add an f to their surnames ending in o. No, they did not resemble those despicable and miserable creatures, but all ancient and native Little Russian families.

It was impossible to behold without sympathy their mutual affection. They never called each other thou, but always you—"You, Afanasii Ivanovich"; "You, Pulcheria Ivanovna."

"Was it you who sold the chair, Afanasii Ivanovich?"

"No matter. Don't you be angry, Pulcheria Ivanovna: it was I."

They never had any children, so all their affection was concentrated upon themselves. At one time, in his youth, Afanasii Ivanovich served in the militia, and was afterwards brevet-major; but that was very long ago, and Afanasii Ivanovich hardly ever thought of it himself. Afanasii Ivanovich married at thirty, while he was still young and wore embroidered waist-coats. He even very cleverly abducted Pulcheria Ivanovna, whose parents did not wish to give her to him. But this, too he recollected very little about; at least, he never mentioned it.

All these long-past and unusual events had given place to a quiet and lonely life, to those dreamy yet harmonious fancies which you experience seated on a country balcony facing the garden, when the beautiful rain patters luxuriously on the leaves, flows the murmuring rivulets, inclining your limbs to repose, and meanwhile the rainbow creeps from behind the trees, and its arch shines dully with its seven hues in the sky; or when your calash rolls on, pushing its way among green bushes, and the quail calls, and the fragrant grass, with the ears of grain and field-flowers, creeps into the door of your carriage, pleasantly striking against your hands and face.

He always listened with a pleasant smile to his guests: sometimes he talked himself but generally he asked questions. He was not one of the old men who weary you with praises of the old times, and complaints of the new: on the contrary, as he put questions to you, he exhibited the greatest curiosity about, and sympathy with, the circumstances of your life, your success, or lack of success, in which kind old men usually are interested; although it closely resembles the curiosity of a child, who examines the seal on your fob while he is asking his questions. Then, it might be said that his face beamed with kindness.

The rooms of the little house in which our old people lived were small, low-studded, such as are generally to be seen with old-fashioned people. In each room stood a huge stove, which occupied nearly one- third of the space. These little rooms were frightfully warm, because both Afanasii Ivanovich and Pulcheria Ivanovna were fond of heat. All their fuel was stored in the vestibule, which was always filled nearly to the ceiling with straw, which is generally used in Little Russia in the place of wood. The crackling and blaze of burning straw render the ante-rooms extremely pleasant on winter evenings, when some lively youth, chilled with his pursuit of some brunette maid, rushes in, beating his hands together.

The walls of the rooms were adorned with pictures in narrow, old-fashioned frames. I am positive that their owners had long ago forgotten their subjects; and, if some of them had been carried off, they probably would not have noticed it. Two of them were large portraits in oil: one represented some bishop; the other, Peter III. From a narrow frame gazed the Duchess of La Vallière, spotted by flies. Around the windows and above the doors were a multitude of small pictures, which you grow accustomed to regard as spots on the wall, and which you never look at. The floor in nearly all the rooms was of clay, but smoothly plastered down, and more cleanly kept than any polished floor of wood in a wealthy house, languidly swept by a sleepy gentleman in livery. Pulcheria Ivanovna's room was all furnished with chests and boxes, and little chests and little boxes. A multitude of little packages and bags, containing seeds—flower-seeds, vegetable-seeds, watermelon-seeds—hung on the walls. A great many balls of various colored woollens, scraps of old dresses, sewed together during half a century, were stuffed away in the riated them. It seemed as though you might read their whole life in them, the pure, peaceful corners, in the chests, and between the chests. Pulcheria Ivanovna was a famous housewife, and saved up every thing; though she sometimes did not know herself what use she could ever make of it.

But the most noticeable thing about the house was the singing doors. Just as soon as day arrived, the songs of the doors resounded throughout the house. I cannot say why they sang. Either the rusty hinges were the cause, or else the mechanic who made them concealed some secret in them; but it was worthy of note, that each door had its own particular voice: the door leading to the bedroom sang the thinnest of sopranos; the dining-room door growled a bass; but the one which led into the vestibule gave out a strange, quavering, yet groaning sound, so that, if you listened to it, you heard at last, quite clearly. "Batiushka [Little Father], I am freezing." I know that this noise is very displeasing to many, but I am very fond of it; and if I chance to hear a door squeak here, I seem to see the country; the low-ceiled chamber, lighted by a candle in an old-fashioned candlestick; the supper on the table; May darkness; night peeping in from the garden through the open windows upon the table set with dishes; the nightingale, which floods the garden, house, and the distant river with her trills; the rustle and the murmuring of the boughs,... and, O God! what a long chain of reminiscences is woven!

The chairs in the room were of wood, and massive, in the style which generally distinguished those of olden times; all had high, turned backs of natural wood, without any paint or varnish; they were not even upholstered, and somewhat resembled those which are still used by bishops. Three-cornered tables stood in the corners, a square one before the sofa; and there was a large mirror in a thin gold frame, carved in leaves, which the flies had covered with black spots; in front of the sofa was a mat with flowers resembling birds, and birds resembling flowers. And this constituted nearly the whole furniture of the far from elegant little house where my old people lived. The maids' room was filled with young and elderly serving-women in striped petticoats, to whom Pulcheria Ivanovna sometimes gave some trifles to sew, and whom she made pick over berries, but who ran about the kitchen or slept the greater part of the time. Pulcheria Ivanovna regarded it as a necessity to keep them in the house; and she looked strictly after their morals, but to no purpose.

Upon the window-panes buzzed a terrible number of flies, overpowered by the heavy bass of the bumble- bee, sometimes accompanied by the penetrating shriek of the wasp; but, as soon as the candles were brought in, this whole horde betook themselves to their night quarters, and covered the entire ceiling with a black cloud.

Afanasii Ivanovich very rarely occupied himself with the farming; although he sometimes went out to the mowers and reapers, and gazed quite intently at their work. All the burden of management devolved upon Pulcheria Ivanovna. Pulcheria Ivanovna's house-keeping consisted of an incessant unlocking and locking of the storeroom, in salting, drying, preserving innumerable quantities of fruits and vegetables. Her house was exactly like a chemical laboratory. A fire was constantly laid under the apple-tree; and the kettle or the brass pan with preserves, jelly, marmalade—made with honey, with sugar, and I know not with what else—was hardly ever removed from the tripod. Under another tree the coachman was forever distilling vodka with peach-leaves, with wild cherry, cherry-flowers, gentian, or cherry-stones in a copper still; and at the end of the process, he never was able to control his tongue, chattered all sorts of nonsense, which Pulcheria Ivanovna did not understand, and took himself off to the kitchen to sleep. Such a quantity of all this stuff was preserved, salted, and dried, that it would probably have overwhelmed the whole yard at last (for Pulcheria Ivanovna loved to lay in a store beyond what was calculated for consumption), if the greater part of it had not been devoured by the maid-servants, who crept into the storeroom, and over-ate themselves to such a fearful extent, that they groaned and complained of their stomachs for a whole day afterwards.

It was less possible for Pulcheria Ivanovna to attend to the agricultural department. The steward conspired with the village elder to rob in the most shameless manner. They had got into a habit of going to their master's forest as though to their own; they manufactured a lot of sledges, and sold them at the neighboring fair; besides which they sold all the stout oaks to the neighboring Cossacks for beams, for a mill. Only once Pulcheria Ivanovna wished to inspect her forest. For this purpose the droshky, with its huge leather apron, was harnessed. As soon as the coachman shook his reins, and the horses (which had served in the militia) started, it filled the air with strange sounds, as though fifes, tambourines, and drums were suddenly audible: every nail and iron bolt rattled so, that, when the pani [mistress] drove from the door, they could be heard clear to the mill, although that was not less than two versts1 away. Pulcheria Ivanovna could not fail to observe the terrible havoc in the forest, and the loss of oaks which she recollected from her childhood as being centuries old. "Why have the oaks become so scarce, Nichípor?" she said to the steward, who was also present. "See that the hairs on your head do not become scarce."

"Why are they scarce?" said the steward. "They disappeared, they disappeared altogether: the lightning struck them, and the worms ate them. They disappeared pani, they disappeared."

Pulcheria Ivanovna was quite satisfied with this answer, and on returning home merely gave orders that double guards should be placed over the Spanish cherries and the large winter-pear trees in the garden.

These worthy managers—the steward and the village elder—considered it quite unnecessary to bring all the flour to the storehouses at the manor, and that half was quite sufficient for the masters, and finally, that half was brought sprinkled or wet through—what had been rejected at the fair. But no matter how the steward and village elder plundered, or how horribly they devoured things at the house, from the housekeeper down to the pigs, who not only made way with frightful quantities of plums and apples, but even shook the trees with their snouts in order to bring down a whole shower of fruit; no matter how the sparrows and crows pecked, or how many presents the servants carried to their friends in other villages, including even old linen and yarn from the storeroom, which all brought up eventually at the universal source, namely, the tavern; no matter how guests, phlegmatic coachmen, and lackeys stole—yet the fruitful earth yielded such an abundance, Afanasii Ivanovich and Pulcheria Ivanovna needed so little, that all this abominable robbery seemed to pass quite unperceived in their household.

Both the old folks, in accordance with old-fashioned customs, were very fond of eating. As soon as daylight dawned (they always rose early), and the doors had begun their many-toned concert, they seated themselves at table, and drank coffee. When Afanasii Ivanovich had drunk his coffee, he went out, and, flirting his handkerchief, said, "Kish, kish! go away from the veranda, geese!" In the yard he generally encountered the steward; he usually entered into conversation with him, inquired about the work with the greatest minuteness, and communicated such a number of observations and orders as would have caused any one to wonder at his knowledge of affairs; and no novice would have ventured to suppose that such an acute master could be robbed. But his steward was a clever rascal: he knew well what answers it was necessary to give, and, better still, how to manage things.

After this, Afanasii Ivanovich returned to the room, and said, approaching Pulcheria Ivanovna, "Well, Pulcheria Ivanovna, is it time to eat something, perhaps?"

"What shall we have to eat now, Afanasii Ivanovich—some wheat and tallow cakes, or some pies with poppy-seeds, or some salted mushrooms?"

"Some mushrooms, then, if you please, or some pies," replied Afanasii Ivanovich; and then suddenly a table-cloth would make its appearance on the table, with the pies and mushrooms.

An hour before dinner, Afanasii Ivanovich took another snack, and drank vodka from an ancient silver cup, ate mushrooms, divers dried fish, and other things. They sat down to dine at twelve o'clock. Besides the dishes and sauce-boats, there stood upon the table a multitude of pots with covers pasted on, that the appetizing products of the savory old-fashioned cooking might not be exhaled abroad. At dinner the conversation turned upon subjects closely connected with the meal.

"It seems to me," Afanasii Ivanovich generally observed, "that this groats is burned a little. Does it strike you so, Pulcheria Ivanovna?"

"No, Afanasii Ivanovich: put on a little more butter, and then it will not taste burned; or take this mushroom sauce, and pour over it."

"If you please," said Afanasii Ivanovich, handing his plate, "let us see how that will do."

After dinner Afanasii Ivanovich went to lie down for an hour, after which Pulcheria Ivanovna brought him a sliced watermelon, and said, "Here, try this, Afanasii Ivanovich; see what a good melon it is."

"Don't trust it because it is red in the centre, Pulcheria Ivanovna," said Afanasii Ivanovich, taking a good- sized chunk. "Sometimes they are red, but not good."

But the watermelon slowly disappeared. Then Afanasii Ivanovich ate a few pears, and went out for a walk in the garden with Pulcheria Ivanovna. On returning to the house Pulcheria went about her own affairs; but he sat down on the veranda facing the yard, and observed how the storeroom's interior was constantly disclosed, and again concealed; and how the girls jostled one another as they carried in, or brought out, all sorts of stuff in wooden boxes, sieves, trays, and other receptacles for fruit. After waiting a while, he sent for Pulcheria Ivanovna, or went to her himself, and said, "What is there for me to eat, Pulcheria Ivanovna?"

"What is there?" said Pulcheria Ivanovna: "shall I go and tell them to bring you some berry tarts which I had set aside for you?"

"That would be good," replied Afanasii Ivanovich.

"Or perhaps you could eat some kissel [sour jelly]?"

"That is good too," replied Afanasii Ivanovich; whereupon all was brought immediately, and eaten in due course.

Before supper Afanasii Ivanovich took another snack. At half-past nine they sat down to supper. After supper they went directly to bed, and universal silence settled down upon this busy yet quiet nook.

The chamber in which Afanasii Ivanovich and Pulcheria Ivanovna slept was so hot that very few people could have stayed in it more than a few hours; but Afanasii Ivanovich, for the sake of more warmth, slept upon the stove-bench, although the excessive heat caused him to rise several times in the course of the night, and walk about the room. Sometimes Afanasii Ivanovich groaned as he walked about the room.

Then Pulcheria Ivanovna inquired, "Why do you groan, Afanasii Ivanovich?"

"God knows, Pulcheria Ivanovna! it seems as if my stomach ached a little," said Afanasii Ivanovich.

"Hadn't you better eat something, Afanasii Ivanovich?"

"I don't know—perhaps it would be well, Pulcheria Ivanovna. By the way, what is there to eat?"

"Sour milk, or some stewed dried pears."

"If you please, I will try them," said Afanasii Ivanovich. The sleepy maid was sent to ransack the cupboards, and Afanasii Ivanovich ate a plateful; after which he remarked, "Now I seem to feel relieved."

Sometimes when the weather was clear, and the rooms were very much heated, Afanasii Ivanovich got merry, and loved to tease Pulcheria Ivanovna, and talk of something out of the ordinary.

"Well, Pulcheria Ivanovna," he said, "what if our house were to suddenly burn down, what would become of us?"

"God forbid!" ejaculated Pulcheria Ivanovna, crossing herself.

"Well, now, just suppose a case, that our house should burn down. Where should we go then?"

"God knows what you are saying, Afanasii Ivanovich! How could our house burn down? God will not permit that."

"Well, but if it did burn?"

"Well, then, we should go to the kitchen. You could occupy for a time the room which the housekeeper now has."

"But if the kitchen burned too?"

"The idea! God will preserve us from such a catastrophe as the house and the kitchen both burning down. In that case, we could go into the store-house while a new house was being built."

"And if the store-house burned also?"

"God knows what you are saying! I won't listen to you! it is a sin to talk so, and God will punish you for such speeches."

But Afanasii Ivanovich, content with having had his joke over Pulcheria Ivanovna, sat quietly in his chair, and smiled.

But the old people were most interesting of all to me when they had visitors. Then everything about their house assumed a different aspect. It may be said that these good people only lived for their guests. They vied with each other in offering you everything which the place produced. But the most pleasing feature of it all to me was, that, in all their kindliness, there was nothing feigned. Their kindness and readiness to oblige were so gently expressed in their faces, so became them, that you involuntarily yielded to their requests. These were the outcome of the pure, clear simplicity of their good, sincere souls. Their joy was not at all of the sort with which the official of the court favors you, when he has become a personage through your exertions, and calls you his benefactor, and fawns at your feet. No guest was ever permitted to depart on the day of his arrival: he must needs pass the night with them.

"How is it possible to set out at so late an hour upon so long a journey!" Pulcheria Ivanovna always observed. (The visitor usually lived three or four versts from them.)

"Of course," said Afanasii Ivanovich, "it is impossible on all accounts; robbers, or some other evil men, will attack you."

"May God in his mercy deliver us from robbers!" said Pulcheria Ivanovna. "And why mention such things at night? Robbers, or no robbers, it is dark, and no fit time to travel. And your coachman,... I know your coachman; he is so weak and small, any horse could kill him; besides, he has probably been drinking, and is now asleep somewhere."

And the visitor was obliged to remain. But the evening in the warm, low room, cheerful, strewn with stories, the steam rising from the food upon the table, which was always nourishing, and cooked in a masterly manner—this was his reward. I seem now to see Afanasii Ivanovich bending to seat himself at the table, with his constant smile, and listening with attention, and even with delight, to his guest. The conversation often turned on politics. The guest, who also emerged but rarely from his village, frequently with significant mien and mysterious expression of countenance, aired his surmises, and told how the French had formed a secret compact with the English to let Buonaparte loose upon Russia again, or talked merely of the impending war; and then Afanasii Ivanovich often remarked, without appearing to look at Pulcheria Ivanovna: "I am thinking of going to the war myself. Why cannot I go to the war?"

"You have been already," broke in Pulcheria Ivanovna. "Don't believe him," she said, turning to the visitor; "what good would he, an old man, do in the war? The very first soldier would shoot him; by Heaven, he would shoot him! he would take aim, and fire at him."

"What?" said Afanasii Ivanovich. "I would shoot him."

"Just listen to him!" interposed Pulcheria Ivanovna. "Why should he go to the war? And his pistols have been rusty this long time, and are lying in the storeroom. If you could only see them! the powder would burst them before they would fire. He will blow his hands off, and disfigure his face, and be miserable forever after!"

"What's that?" said Afanasii Ivanovich. "I will buy myself new arms: I will take my sword or a Cossack lance."

"These are all inventions: as soon as a thing comes into his head, he begins to talk about it!" interrupted Pulcheria Ivanovna with vexation. "I know that he is jesting, but it is unpleasant to hear him all the same. He always talks so; sometimes you listen and listen, until it is perfectly frightful."

But Afanasii Ivanovich, satisfied with having frightened Pulcheria Ivanovna, laughed as he sat doubled up in his chair.

Pulcheria Ivanovna seemed to me most noteworthy when she offered her guest zakuska.2

"Here," she said, taking the cork from a decanter, "is genuine yarrow or sage vodka; if any one's shoulder-blades or loins ache, this is a very good remedy: here is some with gentian; if you have a ringing in your ears, or eruption on your face, this is very good: and this is distilled with peach-kernels; here, take a glass; what a fine perfume! If ever any one, in getting out of bed, strikes himself against the corner of the clothes- press or table, and a bump comes on his forehead, all he has to do is to drink a glass of this before meals—and it all disappears out of hand, as though it had never been." Then followed a catalogue of the other decanters, almost all of which possessed some healing properties. Having loaded down her guest with this complete apothecary shop, she led him to where a multitude of dishes were set out. "Here are mushrooms with summer-savory; and here are some with cloves and walnuts. A Turkish woman taught me how to pickle them, at a time when there were still Turkish prisoners among us. She was a good Turk, and it was not noticeable that she professed the Turkish faith: she behaved very nearly as we do, only she would not eat pork; they say that it is forbidden by their laws. Here are mushrooms with currant-leaves and nutmeg; and here, some with clove-pinks. These are the first I have cooked in vinegar. I don't know how good they are. I learned the secret from Ivan's father: you must first spread oak-leaves in a small cask, and then sprinkle on pepper and saltpetre, and then more, until it becomes the color of hawk-weed, and then spread the liquid over the mushrooms. And here are cheese-tarts; these are different: and here are some pies with cabbage and buckwheat flour, which Afanasii Ivanovich is extremely fond of."

"Yes," added Afanasii Ivanovich, "I am very fond of them; they are soft and a little tart."

Pulcheria Ivanovna was generally in very good spirits when they had visitors. Good old woman! she belonged entirely to her guests. I loved to stay with them; and though I over-ate myself horribly, like all who visited them, and although it was very bad for me, still, I was always glad to go to them. Besides, I think the air of Little Russia must possess some special properties which aid digestion; for if any one undertook to eat here, in that way, there is no doubt but that he would find himself lying on the table instead of in bed.

Good old people!... But my story approaches a very sad event, which changed forever the life in that peaceful nook. This event appears all the more striking because it resulted from the most insignificant cause. But, in accordance with the primitive arrangement of things, the most trifling causes produce the greatest events, and the grandest undertakings end in the most insignificant results. Some warrior collects all the forces of his empire, fights for several years, his colonels distinguish themselves, and at last it all ends in the acquisition of a bit of land on which no one would even plant potatoes; but sometimes, on the other hand, a couple of sausage-makers in different towns quarrel over some trifle, and the quarrel at last extends to the towns, and then to the villages and hamlets, and then to the whole empire. But we will drop these reflections; they lead nowhere: and besides, I am not fond of reflections when they remain mere reflections.

Pulcheria Ivanovna had a little gray cat, which almost always lay coiled up in a ball at her feet. Pulcheria Ivanovna stroked her occasionally, and with her finger tickled her neck, which the petted cat stretched out as long as possible. It was impossible to say that Pulcheria Ivanovna loved her so very much, but she had simply become attached to her from having become used to seeing her about continually. But Afanasii Ivanovich often joked at such an attachment.

"I cannot see, Pulcheria Ivanovna, what you find attractive in that cat; of what use is she? If you had a dog, that would be quite another thing; you can take a dog out hunting, but what is a cat good for?"

"Be quiet, Afanasii Ivanovich," said Pulcheria Ivanovna: "you just like to talk, and that's all. A dog is not clean; a dog soils things and breaks everything: but the cat is a peaceable beast; she does no harm to any one."

But it made no difference to Afanasii Ivanovich whether it was a cat or a dog; he only said it to tease Pulcheria Ivanovna.

Behind their garden was a large wood, which had been spared by the enterprising steward, possibly because the sound of the axe might have reached the ears of Pulcheria Ivanovna. It was dense, neglected: the old tree-trunks were concealed by luxuriant hazel-bushes, and resembled the feathered legs of pigeons. In this wood dwelt wild-cats. The wild forest-cats must not be confounded with those which run about the roofs of houses: being in the city, they are much more civilized, in spite of their savage nature, than the denizens of the woods. These, on the contrary, are mostly fierce and wild: they are always lean and ugly, and miauw in rough, untutored voices. They sometimes scratch for themselves underground passages to the store-houses, and steal tallow. They occasionally make their appearance in the kitchen, springing suddenly in at an open window, when they see that the cook has gone off among the grass. As a rule, noble feelings are unknown to them: they live by thievery, and strangle the little sparrows in their very nests. These cats had a long conference with Pulcheria Ivanovna's tame cat, through a hole under the store-house, and finally led her astray, as a detachment of soldiers leads astray a dull peasant. Pulcheria Ivanovna noticed that her cat was missing, and sent to look for her; but no cat was to be found. Three days passed: Pulcheria Ivanovna felt sorry, but finally forgot all about her loss.

One day she had been inspecting her vegetable-garden, and was returning with her hands full of fresh green cucumbers, which she had picked for Afanasii Ivanovich, when a most pitiful miauwing struck her ear. She instinctively called, "Kitty! kitty!" and out from the tall grass came her gray cat, thin and starved. It was evident that she had not had a mouthful of food for days. Pulcheria Ivanovna continued to call her; but the cat stood crying before her, and did not venture to approach. It was plain that she had become quite wild in that time. Pulcheria Ivanovna stepped forward, still calling the cat, which followed her timidly to the fence. Finally, seeing familiar places, it entered the room.

Pulcheria Ivanovna at once ordered milk and meat to be given her, and, sitting down by her, enjoyed the avidity with which her poor pet swallowed morsel after morsel, and lapped the milk. The gray runaway fattened before her very eyes, and began to eat less eagerly. Pulcheria Ivanovna reached out her hand to stroke her; but the ungrateful animal had evidently become too well used to robber cats, or adopted some romantic notion about love and poverty being better than a palace, for the cats were as poor as church-mice. However that may be, she sprang through the window, and none of the servants were able to catch her.

The old woman reflected. "It is my death which has come for me," she said to herself; and nothing could cheer her. All day she was sad. In vain did Afanasii Ivanovich jest, and want to know why she had suddenly grown so grave. Pulcheria Ivanovna either made no reply, or one which was in no way satisfactory to Afanasii Ivanovich. The next day she was visibly thinner.

"What is the matter with you, Pulcheria Ivanovna? You are not ill?"

"No, I am not ill, Afanasii Ivanovich. I want to tell you about a strange occurrence. I know that I shall die this year: my death has already come for me."

Afanasii Ivanovich's mouth became distorted with pain. Nevertheless, he tried to conquer the sad feeling in his mind, and said, smiling, "God only knows what you are talking about, Pulcheria Ivanovna! You must have drunk some peach infusion instead of your usual herb-tea."

"No, Afanasii Ivanovich, I have not drunk the peach," said Pulcheria Ivanovna.

And Afanasii Ivanovich was sorry that he had made fun of Pulcheria Ivanovna; and as he looked at her, a tear hung on his lashes.

"I beg you, Afanasii Ivanovich, to fulfil my wishes," said Pulcheria Ivanovna. "When I die, bury me by the church-wall. Put my grayish dress on me—the one with small flowers on a cinnamon ground. My satin dress with red stripes, you must not put on me; a corpse needs no clothes. Of what use are they to her? But it will be good for you. Make yourself a fine dressing-gown, in case visitors come, so that you can make a good appearance when you receive them."

"God knows what you are saying, Pulcheria Ivanovna!" said Afanasii Ivanovich. "Death will come some time, but you frighten one with such remarks."

"No, Afanasii Ivanovich: I know when my death is to be. But do not sorrow for me. I am old, and stricken in years; and you, too, are old. We shall soon meet in the other world."

But Afanasii Ivanovich sobbed like a child.

"It is a sin to weep, Afanasii Ivanovich. Do not sin and anger God by your grief. I am not sorry to die: I am only sorry for one thing"—a heavy sob broke her speech for a moment—"I am sorry because I do not know whom I shall leave with you, who will look after you when I am dead. You are like a little child: the one who attends you must love you." And her face expressed such deep and heart-felt sorrow, that I do not know whether any one could have beheld her, and remained unmoved.

"Mind, Yavdokha," she said, turning to the housekeeper, whom she had ordered to be summoned expressly, "that you look after your master when I am dead, and cherish him like the apple of your eye, like your own child. See that everything he likes is prepared in the kitchen; that his linen and clothes are always clean; that, when visitors happen in, you dress him properly: otherwise he will come forth in his old dressing- gown, for he often forgets now whether it is a festival or an ordinary day. Do not take your eyes off him, Yavdokha. I will pray for you in the other world, and God will reward you. Do not forget, Yavdokha. You are old—you have not long to live. Take no sins upon your soul. If you do not look well to him, you will have no happiness in the world. I will beg God myself to give you an unhappy ending. And you will be unhappy yourself, and your children will be unhappy; and none of your race will ever have God's blessing."

Poor old woman! she thought not of the great moment which awaited her, nor of her soul, nor of the future life: she thought only of her poor companion, with whom she had passed her life, and whom she was leaving an orphan and unprotected. After this fashion, she arranged everything with great skill: so that, after her death, Afanasii Ivanovich might not perceive her absence. Her faith in her approaching end was so firm and her mind was so fixed upon it, that, in a few days, she actually took to her bed, and was unable to take any nourishment.

Afanasii Ivanovich was all attention, and never left her bedside. "Perhaps you could eat something, Pulcheria Ivanovna," he said, looking uneasily into her eyes. But Pulcheria Ivanovna made no reply. At length, after a long silence, she moved her lips, as though desirous of saying something—and her breath fled.

Afanasii Ivanovich was utterly amazed. It seemed to him so terrible, that he did not even weep. He gazed at her with troubled eyes, as though he did not comprehend the meaning of a corpse.

They laid the dead woman on a table, dressed her in the dress she herself had designated, crossed her arms, and placed a wax candle in her hand. He looked on without feeling. A throng of people of every class filled the court. Long tables were spread in the yard, and covered with heaps of kutya,3

fruit-wine, and pies. The visitors talked, wept, looked at the dead woman, discussed her qualities, gazed at him; but he looked upon it all as a stranger might. At last they carried out the dead woman: the people thronged after, and he followed. The priests were in full vestments, the sun shone, the infants cried in their mothers' arms, the larks sang, the children in their little blouses ran and capered along the road. Finally they placed the coffin over the grave. They bade him approach and kiss the dead woman for the last time. He approached, and kissed her. Tears appeared in his eyes, but unfeeling tears. The coffin was lowered: the priest took the shovel, and flung in the first earth. The full choir of deacons and two sacristans sang the requiem under the blue, cloudless sky. The laborers grasped their shovels; and the grave was soon filled, the earth levelled off. Then he pressed forward. All stood aside to make room for him, wishing to know his object. He raised his eyes, looked about in a bewildered way, and said, "And so you have buried her! Why?"—He paused, and did not finish his sentence. But when he returned home, when he saw that his chamber was empty, that even the chair on which Pulcheria Ivanovna was wont to sit had been carried out, he sobbed, sobbed violently, irrepressibly; and tears ran in streams from his dim eyes.

Five years passed. What grief will time not efface! What passion is not cured in unequal battle with it! I knew a man in the bloom of his youthful strength, full of true nobility and worth; I knew that he loved, tenderly, passionately, wildly, boldly, modestly; and in my presence, before my very eyes, almost, the object of his passion—a girl, gentle, beautiful as an angel—was struck by insatiable Death. I never beheld such a terrible outburst of spiritual suffering, such mad, fiery grief, such consuming despair, as agitated the unfortunate lover. I never thought that a man could make for himself such a hell, where there was neither shadow nor form, nor any thing in any way resembling hope.... They tried never to let him out of sight: they concealed all weapons from him by which he could commit suicide. Two weeks later he regained control of himself; he began to laugh and jest; they gave him his freedom, and the first use he made of it was to buy a pistol. One day a sudden shot startled his relatives terribly: they rushed into the room, and beheld him stretched out, with his skull crushed. A physician who chanced to be present, and who enjoyed a universal reputation for skill, discovered some signs of life in him, found that the wound was not fatal; and he was cured, to the great amazement of all. The watchfulness over him was redoubled; even at table, they never put a knife near him, and tried to keep everything away from him with which he could injure himself. But he soon found a fresh opportunity, and threw himself under the wheels of a passing carriage. His hand and feet were crushed, but again he was cured. A year after this I saw him in a crowded salon. He was talking gayly, as he covered a card; and behind him, leaning upon the back of his chair, stood his young wife, turning over his counters.

Being in the vicinity during the course of the five years already mentioned, which succeeded Pulcheria Ivanovna's death, I went to the little farm of Afanasii Ivanovich, to inquire after my old neighbor, with whom I had formerly spent the day so agreeably, dining always on the choicest delicacies of his kind- hearted wife. When I drove up to the door, the house seemed twice as old; the peasants' izbás were lying completely on one side, without doubt, exactly like their owners; the fence and hedge around the courtyard were completely dilapidated; and I myself saw the cook pull out a paling to heat the stove, when she had only a couple of steps to take in order to get the kindling-wood which had been piled there expressly. I stepped sadly upon the veranda: the same dogs, now blind, or with broken legs, raised their bushy tails, all matted with burs, and barked.

The old man came out to meet me. So, this was he! I recognized him at once, but he was twice as bent as formerly. He knew me, and greeted me with the smile already so well known to me. I followed him into the room. All there seemed the same as in the past; but I observed a sort of strange disorder, a tangible absence of something: in a word, I experienced that strange sensation which takes possession of us when we enter, for the first time, the dwelling of a widower whom we had heretofore known as inseparable from the companion who has been with him all his life. This sensation resembles the one we feel when we see before us a man whom we had always known as healthy, without his legs. In everything was visible the absence of painstaking Pulcheria Ivanovna. At table they gave us a knife without a handle: the dishes were not prepared with so much art. I did not care to inquire about the management of the estate: I was even afraid to glance at the farm-buildings.

When we sat down at the table, a maid fastened a napkin in front of Afanasii Ivanovich; and it was very well that she did so, for otherwise he would have spotted his dressing-gown all over with gravy. I tried to interest him in something, and told him various bits of news. He listened with his usual smile, but his glance was at times quite unintelligent; and thoughts did not wander there, but only disappeared. He frequently raised a spoonful of porridge, and, instead of carrying it to his mouth, carried it to his nose; and, instead of sticking his fork into the chicken, he struck the decanter with it; and then the servant, taking his hand, guided it to the chicken. We sometimes waited several minutes for the next course. Afanasii Ivanovich remarked it himself, and said, "Why are they so long in bringing the food?" But I saw through a crack of the door that the boy who brought the dishes was not thinking of it at all, but was fast asleep, with his head leaning on a stool.

"This is the dish," said Afanasii Ivanovich, when they brought us mnishki [curds and flour] with cream—"this is the dish," he continued, and I observed that his voice began to quiver, and that tears were ready to peep from his leaden eyes; but he collected all his strength, striving to repress them: "This is the dish which the—the—the de—ceas"—and the tears suddenly burst forth: his hand fell upon the plate, the plate was overturned, flew from the table, and was broken; the gravy ran all over him. He sat stupidly holding his spoon, and tears like a never-ceasing fountain flowed, flowed in streams down upon his napkin.

"O God!" I thought, as I looked at him, "five years of all-obliterating time,... an old man, an already apathetic old man, who, in all his life, apparently, was never agitated by any strong spiritual emotion, whose whole life seemed to consist in sitting on a high chair, in eating dried fish and pears, in telling good-natured stories—and yet so long and fervent a grief! Which wields the most powerful sway over us, passion or habit? Or are all our strong impulses, all the whirlwinds of our desire and boiling passions, but the consequence of our fierce young growth, and only for that reason seem deep and annihilating?" However that may be, all our passion, on that occasion, seemed to me child's play beside this long, slow, almost insensible habit. Several times he tried to pronounce the dead woman's name; but in the middle of the word his peaceful and ordinary face became convulsively distorted, and a childlike fit of weeping cut me to the heart.

No: these were not the tears of which old people are generally so lavish, when representing to us their wretched condition and unhappiness. Neither were these the tears which they drop over a glass of punch. No: these were tears which flowed without asking a reason, distilled from the bitter pain of a heart already growing cold.

He did not live long after this. I heard of his death recently. It was strange, though, that the circumstances attending his death somewhat resembled those of Pulcheria Ivanovna's. One day Afanasii Ivanovich decided to take a short stroll in the garden. As he went slowly down the path, with his usual carelessness, a strange thing happened to him. All at once he heard some one behind him say, in a distinct voice, "Afanasii Ivanovich." He turned round, but there was no one there. He looked on all sides: he peered into the shrubbery—no one anywhere. The day was calm, and the sun shone clear. He pondered for a moment. His face lighted up; and at length he exclaimed, "It is Pulcheria Ivanovna calling me!"

It has doubtless happened to you, at some time or other, to hear a voice calling you by name, which the peasants explain by saying that a man's spirit is longing for him, and calls him, and that death inevitably follows. I confess that this mysterious call has always been very terrifying to me. I remember to have often heard it in my childhood. Sometimes some one suddenly pronounced my name distinctly behind me. The day, on such occasions, was usually bright and sunny. Not a leaf on a tree moved. The silence was deathlike: even the grasshoppers had ceased to whir. There was not a soul in the garden. But I must confess, that, if the wildest and most stormy night, with the utmost inclemency of the elements, had overtaken me alone in the midst of an impassable forest, I should not have been so much alarmed by it as by this fearful stillness amid a cloudless day. On such occasions, I usually ran in the greatest terror, catching my breath, from the garden, and only regained composure when I encountered some person, the sight of whom dispelled the terrible inward solitude.

He yielded himself up utterly to his moral conviction that Pulcheria Ivanovna was calling him. He yielded with the will of a submissive child, withered away, coughed, melted away like a candle and at length expired like it, when nothing remains to feed its poor flame. "Lay me beside Pulcheria Ivanovna"—that was all he said before his death.

His wish was fulfilled; and they buried him beside the church, close to Pulcheria Ivanovna's grave. The guests at the funeral were few, but there was a throng of common and poor people. The house was already quite deserted. The enterprising clerk and village elder carried off to their izbás all the old household utensils and things which the housekeeper did not manage to appropriate

There shortly appeared, from some unknown quarter, a distant relative, the heir of the property, who had served as lieutenant in some regiment, I forget which, and was a great reformer. He immediately perceived the great waste and neglect in the management. This decided him to root out, re-arrange, and introduce order into everything. He purchased six fine English scythes, nailed a number on each izbá, and finally managed so well, that in six months the estate was in the hands of trustees. The wise trustees (consisting of an ex-assessor and a captain of the staff in faded uniform) promptly carried off all the hens and eggs. The izbás, nearly all of which were lying on the ground, fell into complete ruin. The muzhiks wandered off, and were mostly numbered among the runaways. The real owner himself (who lived on peaceable terms with his trustees, and drank punch with them) very rarely entered his village, and did not long live there. From that time forth, he has been going about to all the fairs in Little Russia, carefully inquiring prices at various large establishments, which sell at wholesale, flour, hemp, honey, and so forth, but he buys only the smallest trifles, such as a flint, a nail to clean his pipe, or anything, the value of which at wholesale does not exceed a ruble.

The Calash

THE town of B — — had become very lively since a cavalry regiment had taken up its quarters in it. Up to that date it had been mortally wearisome there. When you happened to pass through the town and glanced at its little mud houses with their incredibly gloomy aspect, the pen refuses to express what you felt. You suffered a terrible uneasiness as if you had just lost all your money at play, or had committed some terrible blunder in company. The plaster covering the houses, soaked by the rain had fallen away in many places from their walls, which from white had become streaked and spotted, whilst old reeds served to thatch them.

Following a custom very common in the towns of South Russia, the chief of police has long since had all the trees in the gardens cut down to improve the view. One never meets anything in the town, unless it is a cock crossing the road, full of dust and soft as a pillow. At the slightest rain this dust is turned into mud, and then all the streets are filled with pigs. Displaying to all their grave faces, they utter such grunts that travellers only think of pressing their horses to get away from them as soon as possible. Sometimes some country gentleman of the neighbourhood, the owner of a dozen serfs, passes in a vehicle which is a kind of compromise between a carriage and a cart, surrounded by sacks of flour, and whipping up his bay mare with her colt trotting by her side. The aspect of the market-place is mournful enough. The tailor's house sticks out very stupidly, not squarely to the front but sideways. Facing it is a brick house with two windows, unfinished for fifteen years past, and further on a large wooden market-stall standing by itself and painted mud-colour. This stall, which was to serve as a model, was built by the chief of police in the time of his youth, before he got into the habit of falling asleep directly after dinner, and of drinking a kind of decoction of dried gooseberries every evening. All around the rest of the market-place are nothing but palings. But in the centre are some little sheds where a packet of round cakes, a stout woman in a red dress, a bar of soap some pounds of bitter almonds, some lead, some cotton and two shopmen playing at ``svaika, *a game resembling quoits, are always to be seen.*

But on the arrival of the cavalry regiment everything changed. The streets became more lively and wore quite another aspect. Often from their little houses the inhabitants would see a tall and well-made officer with a plumed hat pass by, on his way to the quarters of one of his comrades to discuss the chances of promotion or the qualities of a new tobacco, or perhaps to risk at play his carriage, which might indeed be called the carriage of all the regiment, since it belonged in turn to every one of them. To-day it was the major who drove out in it, to-morrow it was seen in the lieutenant's coach-house, and a week later the major's servant was again greasing its wheels. The long hedges separating the houses were suddenly covered with soldiers' caps exposed to the sun, grey frieze cloaks hung in the doorways, and moustaches harsh and bristling as clothes brushes were to be met with in all the streets. These moustaches showed themselves everywhere, but above all at the market, over the shoulders of the women of the place who flocked there from all sides to make their purchases. The officers lent great animation to society at B — — .

Society consisted up till then of the judge who was living with a deacon's wife, and of the chief of police, a very sensible man, but one who slept all day long from dinner till evening, and from evening till dinner-time.

This general liveliness was still further increased when the town of B — — became the residence of the general commanding the brigade to which the regiment belonged. Many gentlemen of the neighbourhood, whose very existence no one had even suspected, began to come into the town with the intention of calling on the officers, or, perhaps, of playing bank, a game concerning which they had up till then only a very confused notion occupied as they were with their crops and the commissions of their wives and their hare-hunting. I am very sorry that I cannot recollect for what reason the general made up his mind one fine day to give a grand dinner. The preparations were overwhelming. The clatter of knives in the kitchen was heard as far as the town gates. The whole of the market was laid under contributions, so much so that the judge and the deacon's wife found themselves obliged that day to be satisfied with hasty pudding and cakes of flour. The little courtyard of the house occupied by the general was crowded with vehicles. The company only consisted of men, officers and gentlemen of the neighbourhood.

Amongst these latter was above all conspicuous Pythagoras Pythagoravitch Tchertokoutski, one of the leading aristocrats of the district of B — — , the most fiery orator at the nobiliary elections and the owner of a very elegant turn-out. He had served in a cavalry regiment and had even passed for one of its most accomplished officers, having constantly shown himself at all the balls and parties wherever his regiment was quartered. Information respecting him may be asked of all the young ladies in the districts of Tamboff and Simbirsk. He would very probably have further extended his reputation in other districts if he had not been obliged to leave the service in consequence of one of those affairs which are spoken of as ``a very unpleasant business. *Had he given or received a blow? I cannot say with certainty, but what is indisputable is that he was asked to send in his resignation.*

However, this accident had no unpleasant effect upon the esteem in which he had been held up till then.

Tchertokoutski always wore a coat of a military cut, spurs and moustache, in order not to have it supposed that he had served in the infantry, a branch of the service upon which he lavished the most contemptuous expressions. He frequented the numerous fairs to which flock the whole of the population of Southern Russia, consisting of nursemaids, tall girls, and burly gentlemen who go there in vehicles of such strange aspect that no one has ever seen their match even in a dream. He instinctively guessed the spot in which a regiment of cavalry was to be found and never failed to introduce himself to the officers. On perceiving them he bounded gracefully from his light phaeton and soon made acquaintance with them. At the last election he had given to the whole of the nobility a grand dinner during which he declared that if he were elected marshal he would put all gentlemen on the best possible footing. He usually behaved after the fashion of a great noble. He had married a rather pretty lady with a dowry of two hundred serfs and some thousands of rubles. This money was at once employed in the purchase of six fine horses, some gilt bronze locks, and a tame monkey. He further engaged a French cook. The two hundred peasants of the lady, as well as two hundred more belonging to the gentleman, were mortgaged to the bank. In a word, he was a regular nobleman. Besides himself, several other gentlemen were amongst the general's guests, but it is not worth while speaking of them. The officers of the regiment, amongst whom were the colonel and the fat major, formed the majority of those present. The general himself was rather stout; a good officer, nevertheless, according to his subordinates. He had a rather deep bass voice.

The dinner was magnificent; there were sturgeons, sterlets, bustards, asparagus, quail, partridges, mushrooms. The flavour of all these dishes supplied an irrefutable proof of the sobriety of the cook during the twenty-four hours preceding the dinner. Four soldiers, who had been given him as assistants, had not ceased working all night, knife in hand, at the composition of ragouts and jellies. The immense quantity of long-necked bottles, mingled with shorter ones, holding claret and madeira; the fine summer day, the wide-open windows, the plates piled up with ice on the table, the crumpled shirt-fronts of the gentlemen in plain clothes, and a brisk and noisy conversation, now dominated by the general's voice, and now besprinkled with champagne, were all in perfect harmony. The guests rose from the table with a pleasant feeling of repletion, and, after having lit their pipes, all stepped out, coffee-cups in hand, on to the verandah.

"We can see her now, *said the general.* ``Here, *my dear fellow,* added he, addressing his aide-de-camp, an active well-made young officer, ``have the bay mare brought here. You shall see for yourselves, gentlemen.

At these words the general took a long pull at his pipe.

"She is not quite recovered yet; there is not a decent stable in this cursed little place. But she is not bad looking — *puff* — *puff, the general here let out the smoke which he had kept in his mouth till then* — ``the little mare.

"Is it long since your excellency — *puff* — *puff* — *puff* — ``condescended to buy her? asked Tchertokoutski.

Puff — puff — puff — puff. ``Not very long, I had her from the breeding establishment two years ago.

"And did your excellency condescend to take her ready broken, or to have her broken in here yourself?

Puff — puff — puff — puff. ``Here.

As he spoke the general disappeared behind a cloud of smoke.

At that moment a soldier jumped out of the stable. The trampling of a horse's hoofs was heard, and another soldier with immense moustaches, and wearing a long white tunic, appeared, leading by the bridle the terrified and quivering mare, which, suddenly rearing lifted him off his feet.

"Come, come, Agrafena Ivanovna, *said he, leading her towards the verandah.*

The mare's name was Agrafena Ivanovna. Strong and bold as a Southern beauty, she suddenly became motionless.

The general began to look at her with evident satisfaction, and left off smoking. The colonel himself went down the steps and patted her neck. The major ran his hand down her legs, and all the other officers clicked their tongues at her.

Tchertokoutski left the verandah to take up a position beside the mare. The soldier who held her bridle drew himself up and stared fixedly at the guests.

"She is very fine, very fine, *said Tchertokoutski ``a very well-shaped beast. Will your excellency allow me to ask whether she is a good goer?*

"She goes well, but that idiot of a doctor, deuce take him, has given her some balls which have made her sneeze for the last two days.

"She is a fine beast, a very fine beast. Has your excellency a turn-out to match the horse?

"Turn-out! but she's a saddle horse.

"I know. I put the question, your excellency, to know if you have an equipage worthy of your other horses?

"No, I have not much in the way of equipages; I must admit that, for some time past, I have been wanting to buy a calash, such as they build now-a-days I have written about it to my brother who is now at St. Petersburg, but I do not know whether he will be able to send me one.

"It seems to me, your excellency, *remarked the colonel, ``that there are no better calashes than those of Vienna.*

"You are right. *Puff — puff — puff.*

"I have an excellent calash, your excellency, a real Viennese calash, *said Tchertokoutski.*

"That in which you came?

"Oh no, I make use of that for ordinary service, but the other is something extraordinary. It is as light as a feather, and if you sit in it, it seems as if your nurse was rocking you in a cradle.

"It is very comfortable then?

"Extremely comfortable; the cushions, the springs, and everything else are perfect.

"Ah! that is good.

"And what a quantity of things can be packed away in it. I have never seen anything like it, your excellency. When I was still in the service there was room enough in the body to stow away ten bottles of rum, twenty pounds of tobacco, six uniforms, and two pipes, the longest pipes imaginable, your excellency; and in the pockets inside you could stow away a whole bullock.

"That is very good.

"It cost four thousand rubles, your excellency.

"It ought to be good at that price. Did you buy it yourself?

"No, your excellency, I had it by chance. It was bought by one of my oldest friends, a fine fellow with whom you would be very well pleased. We are very intimate. What is mine is his, and what is his is mine. I won it of him at cards. Would your excellency have the kindness to honour me at dinner to-morrow? You could see my calash.

"I don't know what to say. Alone I could not — but if you would allow me to come with these officers — —

"I beg of them to come too. I shall esteem it a great honour, gentlemen, to have the pleasure of seeing you at my house.

The colonel, the major, and the other officers thanked Tchertokoutski.

"I am of opinion myself, your excellency, that if one buys anything it should be good; it is not worth the trouble of getting, if it turns out bad. If you do me the honour of calling on me to-morrow, I will show you some improvements I have introduced on my estate.

The general looked at him, and puffed out a fresh cloud of smoke.

Tchertokoutski was charmed with his notion of inviting the officers, and mentally ordered in advance all manner of dishes for their entertainment. He smiled at these gentlemen, who on their part appeared to increase their show of attention towards him, as was noticeable from the expression of their eyes and the little half-nods they bestowed upon him. His bearing assumed a certain ease, and his voice expressed his great satisfaction.

"Your excellency will make the acquaintance of the mistress of the house.

"That will be most agreeable to me, *said the general twirling his moustache.*

Tchertokoutski was firmly resolved to return home at once in order to make all necessary preparations in good time. He had already taken his hat, but a strange fatality caused him to remain for some time at the general's. The card tables had been set out, and all the company, separating into groups of four, scattered itself about the room. Lights were brought in. Tchertokoutski did not know whether he ought to sit down to whist. But as the officers invited him, he thought that the rules of good breeding obliged him to accept. He sat down. I do not know how a glass of punch found itself at his elbow, but he drank it off without thinking. After playing two rubbers, he found another glass close to his hand which he drank off in the same way, though not without remarking:

"It is really time for me to go, gentlemen.

He began to play a fresh rubber. However, the conversation which was going on in every corner of the room took an especial turn. Those who were playing whist were quiet enough, but the others talked a great deal. A captain had taken up his position on a sofa and leaning against a cushion, pipe in mouth, he captivated the attention of a circle of guests gathered about him by his eloquent narrative of amorous adventures.

A very stout gentleman whose arms were so short that they looked like two potatoes hanging by his sides, listened to him with a very satisfied expression, and from time to time exerted himself to pull his tobacco pouch out of his coat-tail pocket. A somewhat brisk discussion on cavalry drill had arisen in another corner, and Tchertokoutski, who had twice already played a knave for a king, mingled in the conversation by calling out from his place: ``In what year? or ``What regiment? without noticing that very often his question had no application whatever. At length, a few minutes before supper, play came to an end. Tchertokoutski could remember that he had won a great deal, but he did not take up his winnings, and after rising stood for some time in the position of a man who has no handkerchief in his pocket.

They sat down to supper. As might be expected, wine was not lacking, and Tchertokoutski kept involuntarily filling his glass with it, for he was surrounded with bottles. A lengthy conversation took place at table, but the guests carried it on after a strange fashion. A colonel, who had served in 1812, described a battle which had never taken place; and besides, no one ever could make out why he took a cork and stuck it into a pie. They began to break-up at three in the morning. The coachmen were obliged to take several of them in their arms like bundles; and Tchertokoutski himself, despite his aristocratic pride, bowed so low to the company, that he took home two thistles in his moustache.

The coachman who drove him home found every one asleep. He routed out, after some trouble, the valet, who, after having ushered his master through the hall, handed him over to a maid-servant. Tchertokoutski followed her as well as he could to the best room, and stretched himself beside his pretty young wife, who was sleeping in a night-gown as white as snow. The shock of her husband falling on the bed awoke her — she stretched out her arms, opened her eyes, closed them quickly, and then opened them again quite wide, with a half-vexed air. Seeing that her husband did not pay the slightest attention to her, she turned over on the other side, rested her fresh and rosy cheek on her hand and went to sleep again.

It was late — that is, according to country customs — when the lady woke again. Her husband was snoring more loudly than ever. She recollected that he had come home at four o'clock, and not wishing to awaken him got up alone, and put on her slippers, which her husband had had sent for her from St. Petersburg, and a white dressing-gown which fell about her like the waters of a fountain. Then she passed into her dressing-room, and after washing in water as fresh as herself, went to her toilet table. She looked at herself twice in the glass, and thought she looked very pretty that morning. This circumstance, a very insignificant one apparently, caused her to stay two hours longer than usual before her glass. She dressed herself very tastefully and went into the garden.

The weather was splendid: it was one of the finest days of the summer. The sun, which had almost reached the meridian, shed its most ardent rays; but a pleasant coolness reigned under the leafy arcades, and the flowers, warmed by the sun, exhaled their sweetest perfume. The pretty mistress of the house had quite forgotten that it was noon at least, and that her husband was still asleep. Already she heard the snores of two coachmen and a groom, who were taking their siesta in the stable, after having dined copiously. But she was still sitting in a bower from which the deserted high road could be seen, when all at once her attention was caught by a light cloud of dust rising in the distance. After looking at it for some moments, she ended by making out several vehicles, closely following one another. First came a light calash, with two places, in which was the general, wearing his large and glittering epaulettes, with the colonel. This was followed by another with four places, containing the captain, the aide-de-camp and two lieutenants. Further on, came the celebrated regimental vehicle, the present owner of which was the major, and behind that another in which were packed five officers, one on his comrade's knees, the procession being closed by three more on three fine bays.

"Are they coming here? *thought the mistress of the house.* ``Good heavens, yes! they are leaving the main road.*

She gave a cry, clasped her hands, and ran straight across the flower-beds to her bedroom, where her husband was still sleeping soundly.

"Get up! get up! get up at once, *she cried, pulling him by the arm.*

"What — what's the matter? *murmured Tchertokoutski, stretching his limbs without opening his eyes.*

"Get up, get up. Visitors have come, do you hear? visitors.

"Visitors, what visitors? *After saying these words he uttered a little plaintive grunt like that of a sucking calf:* ``M-m-m. Let me kiss you.

"My dear, get up at once, for heaven's sake. The general has come with all his officers. Ah! goodness, you have got a thistle in your moustache.

"The general! Has he come already? But why the deuce did not they wake me? And the dinner, is the dinner ready?

"What dinner?

"But haven't I ordered a dinner?

"A dinner! You got home at four o'clock in the morning and you did not answer a single word to all my questions. I did not wake you, since you had so little sleep.

Tchertokoutski, his eyes staring out of his head, remained motionless for some moments as though a thunderbolt had struck him. All at once he jumped out of bed in his shirt.

"Idiot that I am, *he exclaimed, clasping his hand to his forehead;* ``I had invited them to dinner. What is to be done? are they far off?

"They will be here in a moment.

"My dear, hide yourself. Ho there, somebody. Hi there, you girl. Come here, you fool; what are you afraid of? The officers are coming here; tell them I am not at home, that I went out early this morning, that I am not coming back. Do you understand? Go and repeat it to all the servants. Be off, quick.

Having uttered these words, he hurriedly slipped on his dressing-gown, and ran off to shut himself up in the coach-house, which he thought the safest hiding-place. But he fancied that he might be noticed in the corner in which he had taken refuge.

"This will be better, *said he to himself, letting down the steps of the nearest vehicle, which happened to be the calash. He jumped inside, closed the door, and, as a further precaution, covered himself with the leather apron. There he remained, wrapped in his dressing-gown, in a doubled-up position.*

During this time the equipages had drawn up before the porch. The general got out of his carriage and shook himself, followed by the colonel, arranging the feathers in his hat. After him came the stout major, his sabre under his arm, and the slim lieutenants, whilst the mounted officers also alighted.

"The master is not at home, *said a servant appearing at the top of a flight of steps.*

"What! not at home; but he is coming home for dinner, is he not?

"No, he is not; he has gone out for the day and will not be back till this time to-morrow.

"Bless me, *said the general;* ``but what the deuce — —

"What a joke, *said the colonel laughing.*

"No, no, such things are inconceivable, *said the general angrily.* ``If he could not receive us, why did he invite us?

"I cannot understand, your excellency, how it is possible to act in such a manner, *observed a young officer.*

"What? *said the general, who always made an*

officer under the rank of captain repeat his remarks twice over.

"I wondered, your excellency, how any one could do such a thing.

"Quite so; if anything has happened he ought to have let us know.

"There is nothing to be done, your excellency, we had better go back home, *said the colonel.*

"Certainly, there is nothing to be done. However, we can see the calash without him; probably he has not taken it with him. Come here, my man.

"What does your excellency want?

"Show us your master's new calash.

"Have the kindness to step this way to the coach-house.

The general entered the coach-house followed by his officers.

"Let me pull it a little forward, your excellency, *said the servant,* ``it is rather dark here.*

"That will do.

The general and his officers walked round the calash, carefully inspecting the wheels and springs.

"There is nothing remarkable about it, *said the general;* ``it is a very ordinary calash.*

"Nothing to look at, *added the colonel;* ``there is absolutely nothing good about it.*

"It seems to me, your excellency, that it is not worth four thousand rubles, *remarked a young officer.*

"What?

"I said, your excellency, that I do not think that it is worth four thousand rubles.

"Four thousand! It is not worth two. Perhaps, however, the inside is well fitted. Unbutton the apron.

And Tchertokoutski appeared before the officers' eyes, clad in his dressing-gown and doubled up in a singular fashion.

"Hullo, there you are, *said the astonished general.*

Then he covered Tchertokoutski up again and went off with his officers.

The Mysterious Portrait

PART I

Nowhere did so many people pause as before the little picture-shop in the Shtchukinui Dvor. This little shop contained, indeed, the most varied collection of curiosities. The pictures were chiefly oil-paintings covered with dark varnish, in frames of dingy yellow. Winter scenes with white trees; very red sunsets, like raging conflagrations, a Flemish boor, more like a turkey-cock in cuffs than a human being, were the prevailing subjects. To these must be added a few engravings, such as a portrait of Khozreff-Mirza in a sheepskin cap, and some generals with three-cornered hats and hooked noses. Moreover, the doors of such shops are usually festooned with bundles of those publications, printed on large sheets of bark, and then coloured by hand, which bear witness to the native talent of the Russian.

On one was the Tzarevna Miliktrisa Kirbitievna; on another the city of Jerusalem. There are usually but few purchasers of these productions, but gazers are many. Some truant lackey probably yawns in front of them, holding in his hand the dishes containing dinner from the cook-shop for his master, who will not get his soup very hot. Before them, too, will most likely be standing a soldier wrapped in his cloak, a dealer from the old-clothes mart, with a couple of penknives for sale, and a huckstress, with a basketful of shoes. Each expresses admiration in his own way. The muzhiks generally touch them with their fingers; the dealers gaze seriously at them; serving boys and apprentices laugh, and tease each other with the coloured caricatures; old lackeys in frieze cloaks look at them merely for the sake of yawning away their time somewhere; and the hucksters, young Russian women, halt by instinct to hear what people are gossiping about, and to see what they are looking at.

At the time our story opens, the young painter, Tchartkoff, paused involuntarily as he passed the shop. His old cloak and plain attire showed him to be a man who was devoted to his art with self-denying zeal, and who had no time to trouble himself about his clothes. He halted in front of the little shop, and at first enjoyed an inward laugh over the monstrosities in the shape of pictures.

At length he sank unconsciously into a reverie, and began to ponder as to what sort of people wanted these productions? It did not seem remarkable to him that the Russian populace should gaze with rapture upon "Eruslanoff Lazarevitch," on "The Glutton" and "The Carouser," on "Thoma and Erema." The delineations of these subjects were easily intelligible to the masses. But where were there purchases for those streaky, dirty oil-paintings? Who needed those Flemish boors, those red and blue landscapes, which put forth some claims to a higher stage of art, but which really expressed the depths of its degradation? They did not appear the works of a self-taught child. In that case, in spite of the caricature of drawing, a sharp distinction would have manifested itself. But here were visible only simple dullness, steady-going incapacity, which stood, through self-will, in the ranks of art, while its true place was among the lowest trades. The same colours, the same manner, the same practised hand, belonging rather to a manufacturing automaton than to a man!

He stood before the dirty pictures for some time, his thoughts at length wandering to other matters. Meanwhile the proprietor of the shop, a little grey man, in a frieze cloak, with a beard which had not been shaved since Sunday, had been urging him to buy for some time, naming prices, without even knowing what pleased him or what he wanted. "Here, I'll take a silver piece for these peasants and this little landscape. What painting! it fairly dazzles one; only just received from the factory; the varnish isn't dry yet. Or here is a winter scene—take the winter scene; fifteen rubles; the frame alone is worth it. What a winter scene!" Here the merchant gave a slight fillip to the canvas, as if to demonstrate all the merits of the winter scene. "Pray have them put up and sent to your house. Where do you live? Here, boy, give me some string!"

"Hold, not so fast!" said the painter, coming to himself, and perceiving that the brisk dealer was beginning in earnest to pack some pictures up. He was rather ashamed not to take anything after standing so long in front of the shop; so saying, "Here, stop! I will see if there is anything I want here!" he stooped and began to pick up from the floor, where they were thrown in a heap, some worn, dusty old paintings. There were old family portraits, whose descendants, probably could not be found on earth; with torn canvas and frames minus their gilding; in short, trash. But the painter began his search, thinking to himself, "Perhaps I may come across something." He had heard stories about pictures of the great masters having been found among the rubbish in cheap print-sellers' shops.

The dealer, perceiving what he was about, ceased his importunities, and took up his post again at the door, hailing the passers-by with, "Hither, friends, here are pictures; step in, step in; just received from the makers!" He shouted his fill, and generally in vain, had a long talk with a rag-merchant, standing opposite, at the door of his shop; and finally, recollecting that he had a customer in his shop, turned his back on the public and went inside. "Well, friend, have you chosen anything?" said he. But the painter had already been standing motionless for some time before a portrait in a large and originally magnificent frame, upon which, however, hardly a trace of gilding now remained.

It represented an old man, with a thin, bronzed face and high cheek-bones; the features seemingly depicted in a moment of convulsive agitation. He wore a flowing Asiatic costume. Dusty and defaced as the portrait was, Tchartkoff saw, when he had succeeded in removing the dirt from the face, traces of the work of a great artist. The portrait appeared to be unfinished, but the power of the handling was striking. The eyes were the most remarkable picture of all: it seemed as though the full power of the artist's brush had been lavished upon them. They fairly gazed out of the portrait, destroying its harmony with their strange liveliness. When he carried the portrait to the door, the eyes gleamed even more penetratingly. They produced nearly the same impression on the public. A woman standing behind him exclaimed, "He is looking, he is looking!" and jumped back. Tchartkoff experienced an unpleasant feeling, inexplicable even to himself, and placed the portrait on the floor.

"Well, will you take the portrait?" said the dealer.

"How much is it?" said the painter.

"Why chaffer over it? give me seventy-five kopeks."

"No."

"Well, how much will you give?"

"Twenty kopeks," said the painter, preparing to go.

"What a price! Why, you couldn't buy the frame for that! Perhaps you will decide to purchase to-morrow. Sir, sir, turn back! Add ten kopeks. Take it, take it! give me twenty kopeks. To tell the truth, you are my only customer to-day, and that's the only reason."

Thus Tchartkoff quite unexpectedly became the purchaser of the old portrait, and at the same time reflected, "Why have I bought it? What is it to me?" But there was nothing to be done. He pulled a twenty-kopek piece from his pocket, gave it to the merchant, took the portrait under his arm, and carried it home. On the way thither, he remembered that the twenty-kopek piece he had given for it was his last. His thoughts at once became gloomy. Vexation and careless indifference took possession of him at one and the same moment. The red light of sunset still lingered in one half the sky; the houses facing that way still gleamed with its warm light; and meanwhile the cold blue light of the moon grew brighter. Light, half-transparent shadows fell in bands upon the ground. The painter began by degrees to glance up at the sky, flushed with a transparent light; and at the same moment from his mouth fell the words, "What a delicate tone! What a nuisance! Deuce take it!" Re-adjusting the portrait, which kept slipping from under his arm, he quickened his pace.

Weary and bathed in perspiration, he dragged himself to Vasilievsky Ostroff. With difficulty and much panting he made his way up the stairs flooded with soap-suds, and adorned with the tracks of dogs and cats. To his knock there was no answer: there was no one at home. He leaned against the window, and disposed himself to wait patiently, until at last there resounded behind him the footsteps of a boy in a blue blouse, his servant, model, and colour-grinder. This boy was called Nikita, and spent all his time in the streets when his master was not at home. Nikita tried for a long time to get the key into the lock, which was quite invisible, by reason of the darkness.

Finally the door was opened. Tchartkoff entered his ante-room, which was intolerably cold, as painters' rooms always are, which fact, however, they do not notice. Without giving Nikita his coat, he went on into his studio, a large room, but low, fitted up with all sorts of artistic rubbish—plaster hands, canvases, sketches begun and discarded, and draperies thrown over chairs. Feeling very tired, he took off his cloak, placed the portrait abstractedly between two small canvasses, and threw himself on the narrow divan. Having stretched himself out, he finally called for a light.

"There are no candles," said Nikita.

"What, none?"

"And there were none last night," said Nikita. The artist recollected that, in fact, there had been no candles the previous evening, and became silent. He let Nikita take his coat off, and put on his old worn dressing-gown.

"There has been a gentleman here," said Nikita.

"Yes, he came for money, I know," said the painter, waving his hand.

"He was not alone," said Nikita.

"Who else was with him?"

"I don't know, some police officer or other."

"But why a police officer?"

"I don't know why, but he says because your rent is not paid."

"Well, what will come of it?"

"I don't know what will come of it: he said, 'If he won't pay, why, let him leave the rooms.' They are both coming again to-morrow."

"Let them come," said Tchartkoff, with indifference; and a gloomy mood took full possession of him.

Young Tchartkoff was an artist of talent, which promised great things: his work gave evidence of observation, thought, and a strong inclination to approach nearer to nature.

"Look here, my friend," his professor said to him more than once, "you have talent; it will be a shame if you waste it: but you are impatient; you have but to be attracted by anything, to fall in love with it, you become engrossed with it, and all else goes for nothing, and you won't even look at it. See to it that you do not become a fashionable artist. At present your colouring begins to assert itself too loudly; and your drawing is at times quite weak; you are already striving after the fashionable style, because it strikes the eye at once. Have a care! society already begins to have its attraction for you: I have seen you with a shiny hat, a foppish neckerchief. . . . It is seductive to paint fashionable little pictures and portraits for money; but talent is ruined, not developed, by that means. Be patient; think out every piece of work, discard your foppishness; let others amass money, your own will not fail you."

The professor was partly right. Our artist sometimes wanted to enjoy himself, to play the fop, in short, to give vent to his youthful impulses in some way or other; but he could control himself withal. At times he would forget everything, when he had once taken his brush in his hand, and could not tear himself from it except as from a delightful dream. His taste perceptibly developed. He did not as yet understand all the depths of Raphael, but he was attracted by Guido's broad and rapid handling, he paused before Titian's portraits, he delighted in the Flemish masters. The dark veil enshrouding the ancient pictures had not yet wholly passed away from before them; but he already saw something in them, though in private he did not agree with the professor that the secrets of the old masters are irremediably lost to us. It seemed to him that the nineteenth century had improved upon them considerably, that the delineation of nature was more clear, more vivid, more close. It sometimes vexed him when he saw how a strange artist, French or German, sometimes not even a painter by profession, but only a skilful dauber, produced, by the celerity of his brush and the vividness of his colouring, a universal commotion, and amassed in a twinkling a funded capital. This did not occur to him when fully occupied with his own work, for then he forgot food and drink and all the world. But when dire want arrived, when he had no money wherewith to buy brushes and colours, when his implacable landlord came ten times a day to demand the rent for his rooms, then did the luck of the wealthy artists recur to his hungry imagination; then did the thought which so often traverses Russian minds, to give up altogether, and go down hill, utterly to the bad, traverse his. And now he was almost in this frame of mind.

"Yes, it is all very well, to be patient, be patient!" he exclaimed, with vexation; "but there is an end to patience at last. Be patient! but what money have I to buy a dinner with to-morrow? No one will lend me any. If I did bring myself to sell all my pictures and sketches, they would not give me twenty kopeks for the whole of them. They are useful; I feel that not one of them has been undertaken in vain; I have learned something from each one. Yes, but of what use is it? Studies, sketches, all will be studies, trial-sketches to the end. And who will buy, not even knowing me by name? Who wants drawings from the antique, or the life class, or my unfinished love of a Psyche, or the interior of my room, or the portrait of Nikita, though it is better, to tell the truth, than the portraits by any of the fashionable artists? Why do I worry, and toil like a learner over the alphabet, when I might shine as brightly as the rest, and have money, too, like them?"

Thus speaking, the artist suddenly shuddered, and turned pale. A convulsively distorted face gazed at him, peeping forth from the surrounding canvas; two terrible eyes were fixed straight upon him; on the mouth was written a menacing command of silence. Alarmed, he tried to scream and summon Nikita, who already was snoring in the ante-room; but he suddenly paused and laughed. The sensation of fear died away in a moment; it was the portrait he had bought, and which he had quite forgotten. The light of the moon illuminating the chamber had fallen upon it, and lent it a strange likeness to life.

He began to examine it. He moistened a sponge with water, passed it over the picture several times, washed off nearly all the accumulated and incrusted dust and dirt, hung it on the wall before him, wondering yet more at the remarkable workmanship. The whole face had gained new life, and the eyes gazed at him so that he shuddered; and, springing back, he exclaimed in a voice of surprise: "It looks with human eyes!" Then suddenly there occurred to him a story he had heard long before from his professor, of a certain portrait by the renowned Leonardo da Vinci, upon which the great master laboured several years, and still regarded as incomplete, but which, according to Vasari, was nevertheless deemed by all the most complete and finished product of his art. The most finished thing about it was the eyes, which amazed his contemporaries; the very smallest, barely visible veins in them being reproduced on the canvas.

But in the portrait now before him there was something singular. It was no longer art; it even destroyed the harmony of the portrait; they were living, human eyes! It seemed as though they had been cut from a living man and inserted. Here was none of that high enjoyment which takes possession of the soul at the sight of an artist's production, no matter how terrible the subject he may have chosen.

Again he approached the portrait, in order to observe those wondrous eyes, and perceived, with terror, that they were gazing at him. This was no copy from Nature; it was life, the strange life which might have lighted up the face of a dead man, risen from the grave. Whether it was the effect of the moonlight, which brought with it fantastic thoughts, and transformed things into strange likenesses, opposed to those of matter-of-fact day, or from some other cause, but it suddenly became terrible to him, he knew not why, to sit alone in the room. He draw back from the portrait, turned aside, and tried not to look at it; but his eye involuntarily, of its own accord, kept glancing sideways towards it. Finally, he became afraid to walk about the room. It seemed as though some one were on the point of stepping up behind him; and every time he turned, he glanced timidly back. He had never been a coward; but his imagination and nerves were sensitive, and that evening he could not explain his involuntary fear. He seated himself in one corner, but even then it seemed to him that some one was peeping over his shoulder into his face. Even Nikita's snores, resounding from the ante-room, did not chase away his fear. At length he rose from the seat, without raising his eyes, went behind a screen, and lay down on his bed. Through the cracks of the screen he saw his room lit up by the moon, and the portrait hanging stiffly on the wall. The eyes were fixed upon him in a yet more terrible and significant manner, and it seemed as if they would not look at anything but himself. Overpowered with a feeling of oppression, he decided to rise from his bed, seized a sheet, and, approaching the portrait, covered it up completely.

Having done this, he lay done more at ease on his bed, and began to meditate upon the poverty and pitiful lot of the artist, and the thorny path lying before him in the world. But meanwhile his eye glanced involuntarily through the joint of the screen at the portrait muffled in the sheet. The light of the moon heightened the whiteness of the sheet, and it seemed to him as though those terrible eyes shone through the cloth. With terror he fixed his eyes more steadfastly on the spot, as if wishing to convince himself that it was all nonsense. But at length he saw—saw clearly; there was no longer a sheet—the portrait was quite uncovered, and was gazing beyond everything around it, straight at him; gazing as it seemed fairly into his heart. His heart grew cold. He watched anxiously; the old man moved, and suddenly, supporting himself on the frame with both arms, raised himself by his hands, and, putting forth both feet, leapt out of the frame. Through the crack of the screen, the empty frame alone was now visible. Footsteps resounded through the room, and approached nearer and nearer to the screen. The poor artist's heart began beating fast. He expected every moment, his breath failing for fear, that the old man would look round the screen at him. And lo! he did look from behind the screen, with the very same bronzed face, and with his big eyes roving about.

Tchartkoff tried to scream, and felt that his voice was gone; he tried to move; his limbs refused their office. With open mouth, and failing breath, he gazed at the tall phantom, draped in some kind of a flowing Asiatic robe, and waited for what it would do. The old man sat down almost on his very feet, and then pulled out something from among the folds of his wide garment. It was a purse. The old man untied it, took it by the end, and shook it. Heavy rolls of coin fell out with a dull thud upon the floor. Each was wrapped in blue paper, and on each was marked, "1000 ducats." The old man protruded his long, bony hand from his wide sleeves, and began to undo the rolls. The gold glittered. Great as was the artist's unreasoning fear, he concentrated all his attention upon the gold, gazing motionless, as it made its appearance in the bony hands, gleamed, rang lightly or dully, and was wrapped up again. Then he perceived one packet which had rolled farther than the rest, to the very leg of his bedstead, near his pillow. He grasped it almost convulsively, and glanced in fear at the old man to see whether he noticed it.

But the old man appeared very much occupied: he collected all his rolls, replaced them in the purse, and went outside the screen without looking at him. Tchartkoff's heart beat wildly as he heard the rustle of the retreating footsteps sounding through the room. He clasped the roll of coin more closely in his hand, quivering in every limb. Suddenly he heard the footsteps approaching the screen again. Apparently the old man had recollected that one roll was missing. Lo! again he looked round the screen at him. The artist in despair grasped the roll with all his strength, tried with all his power to make a movement, shrieked—and awoke.

He was bathed in a cold perspiration; his heart beat as hard as it was possible for it to beat; his chest was oppressed, as though his last breath was about to issue from it. "Was it a dream?" he said, seizing his head with both hands. But the terrible reality of the apparition did not resemble a dream. As he woke, he saw the old man step into the frame: the skirts of the flowing garment even fluttered, and his hand felt plainly that a moment before it had held something heavy.

The moonlight lit up the room, bringing out from the dark corners here a canvas, there the model of a hand: a drapery thrown over a chair; trousers and dirty boots. Then he perceived that he was not lying in his bed, but standing upright in front of the portrait. How he had come there, he could not in the least comprehend. Still more surprised was he to find the portrait uncovered, and with actually no sheet over it. Motionless with terror, he gazed at it, and perceived that the living, human eyes were fastened upon him. A cold perspiration broke out upon his forehead. He wanted to move away, but felt that his feet had in some way become rooted to the earth. And he felt that this was not a dream. The old man's features moved, and his lips began to project towards him, as though he wanted to suck him in. With a yell of despair he jumped back—and awoke.

"Was it a dream?" With his heart throbbing to bursting, he felt about him with both hands. Yes, he was lying in bed, and in precisely the position in which he had fallen asleep. Before him stood the screen. The moonlight flooded the room. Through the crack of the screen, the portrait was visible, covered with the sheet, as it should be, just as he had covered it. And so that, too, was a dream? But his clenched fist still felt as though something had been held in it. The throbbing of his heart was violent, almost terrible; the weight upon his breast intolerable. He fixed his eyes upon the crack, and stared steadfastly at the sheet. And lo! he saw plainly the sheet begin to open, as though hands were pushing from underneath, and trying to throw it off. "Lord God, what is it!" he shrieked, crossing himself in despair—and awoke.

And was this, too, a dream? He sprang from his bed, half-mad, and could not comprehend what had happened to him. Was it the oppression of a nightmare, the raving of fever, or an actual apparition? Striving to calm, as far as possible, his mental tumult, and stay the wildly rushing blood, which beat with straining pulses in every vein, he went to the window and opened it. The cool breeze revived him. The moonlight lay on the roofs and the white walls of the houses, though small clouds passed frequently across the sky. All was still: from time to time there struck the ear the distant rumble of a carriage. He put his head out of the window, and gazed for some time. Already the signs of approaching dawn were spreading over the sky. At last he felt drowsy, shut to the window, stepped back, lay down in bed, and quickly fell, like one exhausted, into a deep sleep.

He awoke late, and with the disagreeable feeling of a man who has been half-suffocated with coal-gas: his head ached painfully. The room was dim: an unpleasant moisture pervaded the air, and penetrated the cracks of his windows. Dissatisfied and depressed as a wet cock, he seated himself on his dilapidated divan, not knowing what to do, what to set about, and at length remembered the whole of his dream. As he recalled it, the dream presented itself to his mind as so oppressively real that he even began to wonder whether it were a dream, whether there were not something more here, whether it were not really an apparition. Removing the sheet, he looked at the terrible portrait by the light of day. The eyes were really striking in their liveliness, but he found nothing particularly terrible about them, though an indescribably unpleasant feeling lingered in his mind. Nevertheless, he could not quite convince himself that it was a dream. It struck him that there must have been some terrible fragment of reality in the vision. It seemed as though there were something in the old man's very glance and expression which said that he had been with him that night: his hand still felt the weight which had so recently lain in it as if some one had but just snatched it from him. It seemed to him that, if he had only grasped the roll more firmly, it would have remained in his hand, even after his awakening.

"My God, if I only had a portion of that money!" he said, breathing heavily; and in his fancy, all the rolls of coin, with their fascinating inscription, "1000 ducats," began to pour out of the purse. The rolls opened, the gold glittered, and was wrapped up again; and he sat motionless, with his eyes fixed on the empty air, as if he were incapable of tearing himself from such a sight, like a child who sits before a plate of sweets, and beholds, with watering mouth, other people devouring them.

At last there came a knock on the door, which recalled him unpleasantly to himself. The landlord entered with the constable of the district, whose presence is even more disagreeable to poor people than is the presence of a beggar to the rich. The landlord of the little house in which Tchartkoff lived resembled the other individuals who own houses anywhere in the Vasilievsky Ostroff, on the St. Petersburg side, or in the distant regions of Kolomna— individuals whose character is as difficult to define as the colour of a threadbare surtout. In his youth he had been a captain and a braggart, a master in the art of flogging, skilful, foppish, and stupid; but in his old age he combined all these various qualities into a kind of dim indefiniteness. He was a widower, already on the retired list, no longer boasted, nor was dandified, nor quarrelled, but only cared to drink tea and talk all sorts of nonsense over it. He walked about his room, and arranged the ends of the tallow candles; called punctually at the end of each month upon his lodgers for money; went out into the street, with the key in his hand, to look at the roof of his house, and sometimes chased the porter out of his den, where he had hidden himself to sleep. In short, he was a man on the retired list, who, after the turmoils and wildness of his life, had only his old-fashioned habits left.

"Please to see for yourself, Varukh Kusmitch," said the landlord, turning to the officer, and throwing out his hands, "this man does not pay his rent, he does not pay."

"How can I when I have no money? Wait, and I will pay."

"I can't wait, my good fellow," said the landlord angrily, making a gesture with the key which he held in his hand. "Lieutenant-Colonel Potogonkin has lived with me seven years, seven years already; Anna Petrovna Buchmisteroff rents the coach-house and stable, with the exception of two stalls, and has three household servants: that is the kind of lodgers I have. I say to you frankly, that this is not an establishment where people do not pay their rent. Pay your money at once, please, or else clear out."

"Yes, if you rented the rooms, please to pay," said the constable, with a slight shake of the head, as he laid his finger on one of the buttons of his uniform.

"Well, what am I to pay with? that's the question. I haven't a groschen just at present."

"In that case, satisfy the claims of Ivan Ivanovitch with the fruits of your profession," said the officer: "perhaps he will consent to take pictures."

"No, thank you, my good fellow, no pictures. Pictures of holy subjects, such as one could hang upon the walls, would be well enough; or some general with a star, or Prince Kutusoff's portrait. But this fellow has painted that muzhik, that muzhik in his blouse, his servant who grinds his colours! The idea of painting his portrait, the hog! I'll thrash him well: he took all the nails out of my bolts, the scoundrel! Just see what subjects! Here he has drawn his room. It would have been well enough had he taken a clean, well-furnished room; but he has gone and drawn this one, with all the dirt and rubbish he has collected. Just see how he has defaced my room! Look for yourself. Yes, and my lodgers have been with me seven years, the lieutenant-colonel, Anna Petrovna Buchmisteroff. No, I tell you, there is no worse lodger than a painter: he lives like a pig—God have mercy!"

The poor artist had to listen patiently to all this. Meanwhile the officer had occupied himself with examining the pictures and studies, and showed that his mind was more advanced than the landlord's, and that he was not insensible to artistic impressions.

"Heh!" said he, tapping one canvas, on which was depicted a naked woman, "this subject is—lively. But why so much black under her nose? did she take snuff?"

"Shadow," answered Tchartkoff gruffly, without looking at him.

"But it might have been put in some other place: it is too conspicuous under the nose," observed the officer. "And whose likeness is this?" he continued, approaching the old man's portrait. "It is too terrible. Was he really so dreadful? Ah! why, he actually looks at one! What a thunder-cloud! From whom did you paint it?"

"Ah! it is from a—" said Tchartkoff, but did not finish his sentence: he heard a crack. It seems that the officer had pressed too hard on the frame of the portrait, thanks to the weight of his constable's hands. The small boards at the side caved in, one fell on the floor, and with it fell, with a heavy crash, a roll of blue paper. The inscription caught Tchartkoff's eye—"1000 ducats." Like a madman, he sprang to pick it up, grasped the roll, and gripped it convulsively in his hand, which sank with the weight.

"Wasn't there a sound of money?" inquired the officer, hearing the noise of something falling on the floor, and not catching sight of it, owing to the rapidity with which Tchartkoff had hastened to pick it up.

"What business is it of yours what is in my room?"

"It's my business because you ought to pay your rent to the landlord at once; because you have money, and won't pay, that's why it's my business."

"Well, I will pay him to-day."

"Well, and why wouldn't you pay before, instead of giving trouble to your landlord, and bothering the police to boot?"

"Because I did not want to touch this money. I will pay him in full this evening, and leave the rooms to-morrow. I will not stay with such a landlord."

"Well, Ivan Ivanovitch, he will pay you," said the constable, turning to the landlord. "But in case you are not satisfied in every respect this evening, then you must excuse me, Mr. Painter." So saying, he put on his three-cornered hat, and went into the ante-room, followed by the landlord hanging his head, and apparently engaged in meditation.

"Thank God, Satan has carried them off!" said Tchartkoff, as he heard the outer door of the ante-room close. He looked out into the ante-room, sent Nikita off on some errand, in order to be quite alone, fastened the door behind him, and, returning to his room, began with wildly beating heart to undo the roll.

In it were ducats, all new, and bright as fire. Almost beside himself, he sat down beside the pile of gold, still asking himself, "Is not this all a dream?" There were just a thousand in the roll, the exterior of which was precisely like what he had seen in his dream. He turned them over, and looked at them for some minutes. His imagination recalled up all the tales he had heard of hidden hoards, cabinets with secret drawers, left by ancestors for their spendthrift descendants, with firm belief in the extravagance of their life. He pondered this: "Did not some grandfather, in the present instance, leave a gift for his grandchild, shut up in the frame of a family portrait?" Filled with romantic fancies, he began to think whether this had not some secret connection with his fate? whether the existence of the portrait was not bound up with his own, and whether his acquisition of it was not due to a kind of predestination?

He began to examine the frame with curiosity. On one side a cavity was hollowed out, but concealed so skilfully and neatly by a little board, that, if the massive hand of the constable had not effected a breach, the ducats might have remained hidden to the end of time. On examining the portrait, he marvelled again at the exquisite workmanship, the extraordinary treatment of the eyes. They no longer appeared terrible to him; but, nevertheless, each time he looked at them a disagreeable feeling involuntarily lingered in his mind.

"No," he said to himself, "no matter whose grandfather you were, I'll put a glass over you, and get you a gilt frame." Then he laid his hand on the golden pile before him, and his heart beat faster at the touch. "What shall I do with them?" he said, fixing his eyes on them. "Now I am independent for at least three years: I can shut myself up in my room and work. I have money for colours now; for food and lodging—no one will annoy and disturb me now. I will buy myself a first-class lay figure, I will order a plaster torso, and some model feet, I will have a Venus. I will buy engravings of the best pictures. And if I work three years to satisfy myself, without haste or with the idea of selling, I shall surpass all, and may become a distinguished artist."

Thus he spoke in solitude, with his good judgment prompting him; but louder and more distinct sounded another voice within him. As he glanced once more at the gold, it was not thus that his twenty-two years and fiery youth reasoned. Now everything was within his power on which he had hitherto gazed with envious eyes, had viewed from afar with longing. How his heart beat when he thought of it! To wear a fashionable coat, to feast after long abstinence, to hire handsome apartments, to go at once to the theatre, to the confectioner's, to . . . other places; and seizing his money, he was in the street in a moment.

First of all he went to the tailor, was clothed anew from head to foot, and began to look at himself like a child. He purchased perfumes and pomades; hired the first elegant suite of apartments with mirrors and plateglass windows which he came across in the Nevsky Prospect, without haggling about the price; bought, on the impulse of the moment, a costly eye-glass; bought, also on the impulse, a number of neckties of every description, many more than he needed; had his hair curled at the hairdresser's; rode through the city twice without any object whatever; ate an immense quantity of sweetmeats at the confectioner's; and went to the French Restaurant, of which he had heard rumours as indistinct as though they had concerned the Empire of China. There he dined, casting proud glances at the other visitors, and continually arranging his curls in the glass. There he drank a bottle of champagne, which had been known to him hitherto only by hearsay. The wine rather affected his head; and he emerged into the street, lively, pugnacious, and ready to raise the Devil, according to the Russian expression. He strutted along the pavement, levelling his eye-glass at everybody. On the bridge he caught sight of his former professor, and slipped past him neatly, as if he did not see him, so that the astounded professor stood stock-still on the bridge for a long time, with a face suggestive of a note of interrogation.

All his goods and chattels, everything he owned, easels, canvas, pictures, were transported that same evening to his elegant quarters. He arranged the best of them in conspicuous places, threw the worst into a corner, and promenaded up and down the handsome rooms, glancing constantly in the mirrors. An unconquerable desire to take the bull by the horns, and show himself to the world at once, had arisen in his mind. He already heard the shouts, "Tchartkoff! Tchartkoff! Tchartkoff paints! What talent Tchartkoff has!" He paced the room in a state of rapture.

The next day he took ten ducats, and went to the editor of a popular journal asking his charitable assistance. He was joyfully received by the journalist, who called him on the spot, "Most respected sir," squeezed both his hands, and made minute inquiries as to his name, birthplace, residence. The next day there appeared in the journal, below a notice of some newly invented tallow candles, an article with the following heading:—

"TCHARTKOFF'S IMMENSE TALENT

"We hasten to delight the cultivated inhabitants of the capital with a discovery which we may call splendid in every respect. All are agreed that there are among us many very handsome faces, but hitherto there has been no means of committing them to canvas for transmission to posterity. This want has now been supplied: an artist has been found who unites in himself all desirable qualities. The beauty can now feel assured that she will be depicted with all the grace of her charms, airy, fascinating, butterfly-like, flitting among the flowers of spring. The stately father of a family can see himself surrounded by his family. Merchant, warrior, citizen, statesman—

hasten one and all, wherever you may be. The artist's magnificent establishment [Nevsky Prospect, such and such a number] is hung with portraits from his brush, worthy of Van Dyck or Titian. We do not know which to admire most, their truth and likeness to the originals, or the wonderful brilliancy and freshness of the colouring. Hail to you, artist! you have drawn a lucky number in the lottery. Long live Andrei Petrovitch!" (The journalist evidently liked familiarity.) "Glorify yourself and us. We know how to prize you. Universal popularity, and with it wealth, will be your meed, though some of our brother journalists may rise against you."

The artist read this article with secret satisfaction; his face beamed. He was mentioned in print; it was a novelty to him: he read the lines over several times. The comparison with Van Dyck and Titian flattered him extremely. The praise, "Long live Andrei Petrovitch," also pleased him greatly: to be spoken of by his Christian name and patronymic in print was an honour hitherto totally unknown to him. He began to pace the chamber briskly, now he sat down in an armchair, now he sprang up, and seated himself on the sofa, planning each moment how he would receive visitors, male and female; he went to his canvas and made a rapid sweep of the brush, endeavouring to impart a graceful movement to his hand.

The next day, the bell at his door rang. He hastened to open it. A lady entered, accompanied by a girl of eighteen, her daughter, and followed by a lackey in a furred livery-coat.

"You are the painter Tchartkoff?"

The artist bowed.

"A great deal is written about you: your portraits, it is said, are the height of perfection." So saying, the lady raised her glass to her eyes and glanced rapidly over the walls, upon which nothing was hanging. "But where are your portraits?"

"They have been taken away" replied the artist, somewhat confusedly: "I have but just moved into these apartments; so they are still on the road, they have not arrived."

"You have been in Italy?" asked the lady, levelling her glass at him, as she found nothing else to point it at.

"No, I have not been there; but I wish to go, and I have deferred it for a while. Here is an arm-chair, madame: you are fatigued?"

"Thank you: I have been sitting a long time in the carriage. Ah, at last I behold your work!" said the lady, running to the opposite wall, and bringing her glass to bear upon his studies, sketches, views and portraits which were standing there on the floor. "It is charming. Lise! Lise, come here. Rooms in the style of Teniers. Do you see? Disorder, disorder, a table with a bust upon it, a hand, a palette; dust, see how the dust is painted! It is charming. And here on this canvas is a woman washing her face. What a pretty face! Ah! a little muzhik! So you do not devote yourself exclusively to portraits?"

"Oh! that is mere rubbish. I was trying experiments, studies."

"Tell me your opinion of the portrait painters of the present day. Is it not true that there are none now like Titian? There is not that strength of colour, that—that— What a pity that I cannot express myself in Russian." The lady was fond of paintings, and had gone through all the galleries in Italy with her eye-glass. "But Monsieur Nohl—ah, how well he paints! what remarkable work! I think his faces have been more expression than Titian's. You do not know Monsieur Nohl?"

"Who is Nohl?" inquired the artist.

"Monsieur Nohl. Ah, what talent! He painted her portrait when she was only twelve years old. You must certainly come to see us. Lise, you shall show him your album. You know, we came expressly that you might begin her portrait immediately."

"What? I am ready this very moment." And in a trice he pulled forward an easel with a canvas already prepared, grasped his palette, and fixed his eyes on the daughter's pretty little face. If he had been acquainted with human nature, he might have read in it the dawning of a childish passion for balls, the dawning of sorrow and misery at the length of time before dinner and after dinner, the heavy traces of uninterested application to various arts, insisted upon by her mother for the elevation of her mind. But the artist saw only the tender little face, a seductive subject for his brush, the body almost as transparent as porcelain, the delicate white neck, and the aristocratically slender form. And he prepared beforehand to triumph, to display the delicacy of his brush, which had hitherto had to deal only with the harsh features of coarse models, and severe antiques and copies of classic masters. He already saw in fancy how this delicate little face would turn out.

"Do you know," said the lady with a positively touching expression of countenance, "I should like her to be painted simply attired, and seated among green shadows, like meadows, with a flock or a grove in the distance, so that it could not be seen that she goes to balls or fashionable entertainments. Our balls, I must confess, murder the intellect, deaden all remnants of feeling. Simplicity! would there were more simplicity!" Alas, it was stamped on the faces of mother and daughter that they had so overdanced themselves at balls that they had become almost wax figures.

Tchartkoff set to work, posed his model, reflected a bit, fixed upon the idea, waved his brush in the air, settling the points mentally, and then began and finished the sketching in within an hour. Satisfied with it, he began to paint. The task fascinated him; he forgot everything, forgot the very existence of the aristocratic ladies, began even to display some artistic tricks, uttering various odd sounds and humming to himself now and then as artists do when immersed heart and soul in their work. Without the slightest ceremony, he made the sitter lift her head, which finally began to express utter weariness.

"Enough for the first time," said the lady.

"A little more," said the artist, forgetting himself.

"No, it is time to stop. Lise, three o'clock!" said the lady, taking out a tiny watch which hung by a gold chain from her girdle. "How late it is!"

"Only a minute," said Tchartkoff innocently, with the pleading voice of a child.

But the lady appeared to be not at all inclined to yield to his artistic demands on this occasion; she promised, however, to sit longer the next time.

"It is vexatious, all the same," thought Tchartkoff to himself: "I had just got my hand in;" and he remembered no one had interrupted him or stopped him when he was at work in his studio on Vasilievsky Ostroff. Nikita sat motionless in one place. You might even paint him as long as you pleased; he even went to sleep in the attitude prescribed him. Feeling dissatisfied, he laid his brush and palette on a chair, and paused in irritation before the picture.

The woman of the world's compliments awoke him from his reverie. He flew to the door to show them out: on the stairs he received an invitation to dine with them the following week, and returned with a cheerful face to his apartments. The aristocratic lady had completely charmed him. Up to that time he had looked upon such beings as unapproachable, born solely to ride in magnificent carriages, with liveried footmen and stylish coachmen, and to cast indifferent glances on the poor man travelling on foot in a cheap cloak. And now, all of a sudden, one of these very beings had entered his room; he was painting her portrait, was invited to dinner at an aristocratic house. An unusual feeling of pleasure took possession of him: he was completely intoxicated, and rewarded himself with a splendid dinner, an evening at the theatre, and a drive through the city in a carriage, without any necessity whatever.

But meanwhile his ordinary work did not fall in with his mood at all. He did nothing but wait for the moment when the bell should ring. At last the aristocratic lady arrived with her pale daughter. He seated them, drew forward the canvas with skill, and some efforts of fashionable airs, and began to paint. The sunny day and bright light aided him not a little: he saw in his dainty sitter much which, caught and committed to canvas, would give great value to the portrait. He perceived that he might accomplish something good if he could reproduce, with accuracy, all that nature then offered to his eyes. His heart began to beat faster as he felt that he was expressing something which others had not even seen as yet. His work engrossed him completely: he was wholly taken up with it, and again forgot the aristocratic origin of the sitter. With heaving breast he saw the delicate features and the almost transparent body of the fair maiden grow beneath his hand. He had caught every shade, the slight sallowness, the almost imperceptible blue tinge under the eyes—and was already preparing to put in the tiny mole on the brow, when he suddenly heard the mother's voice behind him.

"Ah! why do you paint that? it is not necessary: and you have made it here, in several places, rather yellow; and here, quite so, like dark spots."

The artist undertook to explain that the spots and yellow tinge would turn out well, that they brought out the delicate and pleasing tones of the face. He was informed that they did not bring out tones, and would not turn out well at all. It was explained to him that just to-day Lise did not feel quite well; that she never was sallow, and that her face was distinguished for its fresh colouring.

Sadly he began to erase what his brush had put upon the canvas. Many a nearly imperceptible feature disappeared, and with it vanished too a portion of the resemblance. He began indifferently to impart to the picture that commonplace colouring which can be painted mechanically, and which lends to a face, even when taken from nature, the sort of cold ideality observable on school programmes. But the lady was satisfied when the objectionable tone was quite banished. She merely expressed surprise that the work lasted so long, and added that she had heard that he finished a portrait completely in two sittings. The artist could not think of any answer to this. The ladies rose, and prepared to depart. He laid aside his brush, escorted them to the door, and then stood disconsolate for a long while in one spot before the portrait.

He gazed stupidly at it; and meanwhile there floated before his mind's eye those delicate features, those shades, and airy tints which he had copied, and which his brush had annihilated. Engrossed with them, he put the portrait on one side and hunted up a head of Psyche which he had some time before thrown on canvas in a sketchy manner. It was a pretty little face, well painted, but entirely ideal, and having cold, regular features not lit up by life. For lack of occupation, he now began to tone it up, imparting to it all he had taken note of in his aristocratic sitter. Those features, shadows, tints, which he had noted, made their appearance here in the purified form in which they appear when the painter, after closely observing nature, subordinates himself to her, and produces a creation equal to her own.

Psyche began to live: and the scarcely dawning thought began, little by little, to clothe itself in a visible form. The type of face of the fashionable young lady was unconsciously transferred to Psyche, yet nevertheless she had an expression of her own which gave the picture claims to be considered in truth an original creation. Tchartkoff gave himself up entirely to his work. For several days he was engrossed by it alone, and the ladies surprised him at it on their arrival. He had not time to remove the picture from the easel. Both ladies uttered a cry of amazement, and clasped their hands.

"Lise, Lise! Ah, how like! Superb, superb! What a happy thought, too, to drape her in a Greek costume! Ah, what a surprise!"

The artist could not see his way to disabuse the ladies of their error. Shamefacedly, with drooping head, he murmured, "This is Psyche."

"In the character of Psyche? Charming!" said the mother, smiling, upon which the daughter smiled too. "Confess, Lise, it pleases you to be painted in the character of Psyche better than any other way? What a sweet idea! But what treatment! It is Correggio himself. I must say that, although I had read and heard about you, I did not know you had so much talent. You positively must paint me too." Evidently the lady wanted to be portrayed as some kind of Psyche too.

"What am I to do with them?" thought the artist. "If they will have it so, why, let Psyche pass for what they choose:" and added aloud, "Pray sit a little: I will touch it up here and there."

"Ah! I am afraid you will . . . it is such a capital likeness now!"

But the artist understood that the difficulty was with respect to the sallowness, and so he reassured them by saying that he only wished to give more brilliancy and expression to the eyes. In truth, he was ashamed, and wanted to impart a little more likeness to the original, lest any one should accuse him of actual barefaced flattery. And the features of the pale young girl at length appeared more closely in Psyche's countenance.

"Enough," said the mother, beginning to fear that the likeness might become too decided. The artist was remunerated in every way, with smiles, money, compliments, cordial pressures of the hand, invitations to dinner: in short, he received a thousand flattering rewards.

The portrait created a furore in the city. The lady exhibited it to her friends, and all admired the skill with which the artist had preserved the likeness, and at the same time conferred more beauty on the original. The last remark, of course, was prompted by a slight tinge of envy. The artist was suddenly overwhelmed with work. It seemed as if the whole city wanted to be painted by him. The door-bell rang incessantly. From one point of view, this might be considered advantageous, as presenting to him endless practice in variety and number of faces. But, unfortunately, they were all people who were hard to get along with, either busy, hurried people, or else belonging to the fashionable world, and consequently more occupied than any one else, and therefore impatient to the last degree. In all quarters, the demand was merely that the likeness should be good and quickly executed. The artist perceived that it was a simple impossibility to finish his work; that it was necessary to exchange power of treatment for lightness and rapidity, to catch only the general expression, and not waste labour on delicate details.

Moreover, nearly all of his sitters made stipulations on various points. The ladies required that mind and character should be represented in their portraits; that all angles should be rounded, all unevenness smoothed away, and even removed entirely if possible; in short, that their faces should be such as to cause every one to stare at them with admiration, if not fall in love with them outright. When they sat to him, they sometimes assumed expressions which greatly amazed the artist; one tried to express melancholy; another, meditation; a third wanted to make her mouth appear small on any terms, and puckered it up to such an extent that it finally looked like a spot about as big as a pinhead. And in spite of all this, they demanded of him good likenesses and unconstrained naturalness. The men were no better: one insisted on being painted with an energetic, muscular turn to his head; another, with upturned, inspired eyes; a lieutenant of the guard demanded that Mars should be visible in his eyes; an official in the civil service drew himself up to his full height in order to have his uprightness expressed in his face, and that his hand might rest on a book bearing the words in plain characters, "He always stood up for the right."

At first such demands threw the artist into a cold perspiration. Finally he acquired the knack of it, and never troubled himself at all about it. He understood at a word how each wanted himself portrayed. If a man wanted Mars in his face, he put in Mars: he gave a Byronic turn and attitude to those who aimed at Byron. If the ladies wanted to be Corinne, Undine, or Aspasia, he agreed with great readiness, and threw in a sufficient measure of good looks from his own imagination, which does no harm, and for the sake of which an artist is even forgiven a lack of resemblance. He soon began to wonder himself at the rapidity and dash of his brush. And of course those who sat to him were in ecstasies, and proclaimed him a genius.

Tchartkoff became a fashionable artist in every sense of the word. He began to dine out, to escort ladies to picture galleries, to dress foppishly, and to assert audibly that an artist should belong to society, that he must uphold his profession, that artists mostly dress like showmakers, do not know how to behave themselves, do not maintain the highest tone, and are lacking in all polish. At home, in his studio, he carried cleanliness and spotlessness to the last extreme, set up two superb footmen, took fashionable pupils, dressed several times a day, curled his hair, practised various manners of receiving his callers, and busied himself in adorning his person in every conceivable way, in order to produce a pleasing impression on the ladies. In short, it would soon have been impossible for any one to have recognised in him the modest artist who had formerly toiled unknown in his miserable quarters in the Vasilievsky Ostroff.

He now expressed himself decidedly concerning artists and art; declared that too much credit had been given to the old masters; that even Raphael did not always paint well, and that fame attached to many of his works simply by force of tradition: that Michael Angelo was a braggart because he could boast only a knowledge of anatomy; that there was no grace about him, and that real brilliancy and power of treatment and colouring were to be looked for in the present century. And there, naturally, the question touched him personally. "I do not understand," said he, "how others toil and work with difficulty: a man who labours for months over a picture is a dauber, and no artist in my opinion; I don't believe he has any talent: genius works boldly, rapidly. Here is this portrait which I painted in two days, this head in one day, this in a few hours, this in little more than an hour. No, I confess I do not recognise as art that which adds line to line; that is a handicraft, not art." In this manner did he lecture his visitors; and the visitors admired the strength and boldness of his works, uttered exclamations on hearing how fast they had been produced, and said to each other, "This is talent, real talent! see how he speaks, how his eyes gleam! There is something really extraordinary in his face!"

It flattered the artist to hear such reports about himself. When printed praise appeared in the papers, he rejoiced like a child, although this praise was purchased with his money. He carried the printed slips about with him everywhere, and showed them to friends and acquaintances as if by accident. His fame increased, his works and orders multiplied. Already the same portraits over and over again wearied him, by the same attitudes and turns, which he had learned by heart. He painted them now without any great interest in his work, brushing in some sort of a head, and giving them to his pupil's to finish. At first he had sought to devise a new attitude each time. Now this had grown wearisome to him. His brain was tired with planning and thinking. It was out of his power; his fashionable life bore him far away from labour and thought. His work grew cold and colourless; and he betook himself with indifference to the reproduction of monotonous, well-worn forms. The eternally spick-and-span uniforms, and the so-to-speak buttoned-up faces of the government officials, soldiers, and statesmen, did not offer a wide field for his brush: it forgot how to render superb draperies and powerful emotion and passion. Of grouping, dramatic effect and its lofty connections, there was nothing. In face of him was only a uniform, a corsage, a dress-coat, and before which the artist feels cold and all imagination vanishes. Even his own peculiar merits were no longer visible in his works, yet they continued to enjoy renown; although genuine connoisseurs and artists merely shrugged their shoulders when they saw his latest productions.

But some who had known Tchartkoff in his earlier days could not understand how the talent of which he had given such clear indications in the outset could so have vanished; and strove in vain to divine by what means genius could be extinguished in a man just when he had attained to the full development of his powers.

But the intoxicated artist did not hear these criticisms. He began to attain to the age of dignity, both in mind and years: to grow stout, and increase visibly in flesh. He often read in the papers such phrases as, "Our most respected Andrei Petrovitch; our worthy Andrei Petrovitch." He began to receive offers of distinguished posts in the service, invitations to examinations and committees. He began, as is usually the case in maturer years, to advocate Raphael and the old masters, not because he had become thoroughly convinced of their transcendent merits, but in order to snub the younger artists. His life was already approaching the period when everything which suggests impulse contracts within a man; when a powerful chord appeals more feebly to the spirit; when the touch of beauty no longer converts virgin strength into fire and flame, but when all the burnt-out sentiments become more vulnerable to the sound of gold, hearken more attentively to its seductive music, and little by little permit themselves to be completely lulled to sleep by it. Fame can give no pleasure to him who has stolen it, not won it; so all his feelings and impulses turned towards wealth. Gold was his passion, his ideal, his fear, his delight, his aim. The bundles of bank-notes increased in his coffers; and, like all to whose lot falls this fearful gift, he began to grow inaccessible to every sentiment except the love of gold. But something occurred which gave him a powerful shock, and disturbed the whole tenor of his life.

One day he found upon his table a note, in which the Academy of Painting begged him, as a worthy member of its body, to come and give his opinion upon a new work which had been sent from Italy by a Russian artist who was perfecting himself there. The painter was one of his former comrades, who had been possessed with a passion for art from his earliest years, had given himself up to it with his whole soul, estranged himself from his friends and relatives, and had hastened to that wonderful Rome, at whose very name the artist's heart beats wildly and hotly. There he buried himself in his work from which he permitted nothing to entice him. He visited the galleries unweariedly, he stood for hours at a time before the works of the great masters, seizing and studying their marvellous methods. He never finished anything without revising his impressions several times before these great teachers, and reading in their works silent but eloquent counsels. He gave each impartially his due, appropriating from all only that which was most beautiful, and finally became the pupil of the divine Raphael alone, as a great poet, after reading many works, at last made Homer's "Iliad" his only breviary, having discovered that it contains all one wants, and that there is nothing which is not expressed in it in perfection. And so he brought away from his school the grand conception of creation, the mighty beauty of thought, the high charm of that heavenly brush.

When Tchartkoff entered the room, he found a crowd of visitors already collected before the picture. The most profound silence, such as rarely settles upon a throng of critics, reigned over all. He hastened to assume the significant expression of a connoisseur, and approached the picture; but, O God! what did he behold!

Pure, faultless, beautiful as a bride, stood the picture before him. The critics regarded this new hitherto unknown work with a feeling of involuntary wonder. All seemed united in it: the art of Raphael, reflected in the lofty grace of the grouping; the art of Correggio, breathing from the finished perfection of the workmanship. But more striking than all else was the evident creative power in the artist's mind. The very minutest object in the picture revealed it; he had caught that melting roundness of outline which is visible in nature only to the artist creator, and which comes out as angles with a copyist. It was plainly visible how the artist, having imbibed it all from the external world, had first stored it in his mind, and then drawn it thence, as from a spiritual source, into one harmonious, triumphant song. And it was evident, even to the uninitiated, how vast a gulf there was fixed between creation and a mere copy from nature. Involuntary tears stood ready to fall in the eyes of those who surrounded the picture. It seemed as though all joined in a silent hymn to the divine work.

Motionless, with open mouth, Tchartkoff stood before the picture. At length, when by degrees the visitors and critics began to murmur and comment upon the merits of the work, and turning to him, begged him to express an opinion, he came to himself once more. He tried to assume an indifferent, everyday expression; strove to utter some such commonplace remark as; "Yes, to tell the truth, it is impossible to deny the artist's talent; there is something in it;" but the speech died upon his lips, tears and sobs burst forth uncontrollably, and he rushed from the room like one beside himself.

In a moment he stood in his magnificent studio. All his being, all his life, had been aroused in one instant, as if youth had returned to him, as if the dying sparks of his talent had blazed forth afresh. The bandage suddenly fell from his eyes. Heavens! to think of having mercilessly wasted the best years of his youth, of having extinguished, trodden out perhaps, that spark of fire which, cherished in his breast, might perhaps have been developed into magnificence and beauty, and have extorted too, its meed of tears and admiration! It seemed as though those impulses which he had known in other days re-awoke suddenly in his soul.

He seized a brush and approached his canvas. One thought possessed him wholly, one desire consumed him; he strove to depict a fallen angel. This idea was most in harmony with his frame of mind. The perspiration started out upon his face with his efforts; but, alas! his figures, attitudes, groups, thoughts, arranged themselves stiffly, disconnectedly. His hand and his imagination had been too long confined to one groove; and the fruitless effort to escape from the bonds and fetters which he had imposed upon himself, showed itself in irregularities and errors. He had despised the long, wearisome ladder to knowledge, and the first fundamental law of the future great man, hard work. He gave vent to his vexation. He ordered all his later productions to be taken out of his studio, all the fashionable, lifeless pictures, all the portraits of hussars, ladies, and councillors of state.

He shut himself up alone in his room, would order no food, and devoted himself entirely to his work. He sat toiling like a scholar. But how pitifully wretched was all which proceeded from his hand! He was stopped at every step by his ignorance of the very first principles: simple ignorance of the mechanical part of his art chilled all inspiration and formed an impassable barrier to his imagination. His brush returned involuntarily to hackneyed forms: hands folded themselves in a set attitude; heads dared not make any unusual turn; the very garments turned out commonplace, and would not drape themselves to any unaccustomed posture of the body. And he felt and saw this all himself.

"But had I really any talent?" he said at length: "did not I deceive myself?" Uttering these words, he turned to the early works which he had painted so purely, so unselfishly, in former days, in his wretched cabin yonder in lonely Vasilievsky Ostroff. He began attentively to examine them all; and all the misery of his former life came back to him. "Yes," he cried despairingly, "I had talent: the signs and traces of it are everywhere visible—"

He paused suddenly, and shivered all over. His eyes encountered other eyes fixed immovably upon him. It was that remarkable portrait which he had bought in the Shtchukinui Dvor. All this time it had been covered up, concealed by other pictures, and had utterly gone out of his mind. Now, as if by design, when all the fashionable portraits and paintings had been removed from the studio, it looked forth, together with the productions of his early youth. As he recalled all the strange events connected with it; as he remembered that this singular portrait had been, in a manner, the cause of his errors; that the hoard of money which he had obtained in such peculiar fashion had given birth in his mind to all the wild caprices which had destroyed his talent—madness was on the point of taking possession of him. At once he ordered the hateful portrait to be removed.

But his mental excitement was not thereby diminished. His whole being was shaken to its foundation; and he suffered that fearful torture which is sometimes exhibited when a feeble talent strives to display itself on a scale too great for it and cannot do so. A horrible envy took possession of him—an envy which bordered on madness. The gall flew to his heart when he beheld a work which bore the stamp of talent. He gnashed his teeth, and devoured it with the glare of a basilisk. He conceived the most devilish plan which ever entered into the mind of man, and he hastened with the strength of madness to carry it into execution. He began to purchase the best that art produced of every kind. Having bought a picture at a great price, he transported it to his room, flung himself upon it with the ferocity of a tiger, cut it, tore it, chopped it into bits, and stamped upon it with a grin of delight.

The vast wealth he had amassed enabled him to gratify this devilish desire. He opened his bags of gold and unlocked his coffers. No monster of ignorance ever destroyed so many superb productions of art as did this raging avenger. At any auction where he made his appearance, every one despaired at once of obtaining any work of art. It seemed as if an angry heaven had sent this fearful scourge into the world expressly to destroy all harmony. Scorn of the world was expressed in his countenance. His tongue uttered nothing save biting and censorious words. He swooped down like a harpy into the street: and his acquaintances, catching sight of him in the distance, sought to turn aside and avoid a meeting with him, saying that it poisoned all the rest of the day.

Fortunately for the world and art, such a life could not last long: his passions were too overpowering for his feeble strength. Attacks of madness began to recur more frequently, and ended at last in the most frightful illness. A violent fever, combined with galloping consumption, seized upon him with such violence, that in three days there remained only a shadow of his former self. To this was added indications of hopeless insanity. Sometimes several men were unable to hold him. The long-forgotten, living eyes of the portrait began to torment him, and then his madness became dreadful. All the people who surrounded his bed seemed to him horrible portraits. The portrait doubled and quadrupled itself; all the walls seemed hung with portraits, which fastened their living eyes upon him; portraits glared at him from the ceiling, from the floor; the room widened and lengthened endlessly, in order to make room for more of the motionless eyes. The doctor who had undertaken to attend him, having learned something of his strange history, strove with all his might to fathom the secret connection between the visions of his fancy and the occurrences of his life, but without the slightest success. The sick man understood nothing, felt nothing, save his own tortures, and gave utterance only to frightful yells and unintelligible gibberish. At last his life ended in a final attack of unutterable suffering. Nothing could be found of all his great wealth; but when they beheld the mutilated fragments of grand works of art, the value of which exceeded a million, they understood the terrible use which had been made of it

PART II

A THRONG of carriages and other vehicles stood at the entrance of a house in which an auction was going on of the effects of one of those wealthy art-lovers who have innocently passed for Maecenases, and in a simple-minded fashion expended, to that end, the millions amassed by their thrifty fathers, and frequently even by their own early labours. The long saloon was filled with the most motley throng of visitors, collected like birds of prey swooping down upon an unburied corpse. There was a whole squadron of Russian shop-keepers from the Gostinnui Dvor, and from the old-clothes mart, in blue coats of foreign make. Their faces and expressions were a little more natural here, and did not display that fictitious desire to be subservient which is so marked in the Russian shop-keeper when he stands before a customer in his shop. Here they stood upon no ceremony, although the saloons were full of those very aristocrats before whom, in any other place, they would have been ready to sweep, with reverence, the dust brought in by their feet. They were quite at their ease, handling pictures and books without ceremony, when desirous of ascertaining the value of the goods, and boldly upsetting bargains mentally secured in advance by noble connoisseurs. There were many of those infallible attendants of auctions who make it a point to go to one every day as regularly as to take their breakfast; aristocratic connoisseurs who look upon it as their duty not to miss any opportunity of adding to their collections, and who have no other occupation between twelve o'clock and one; and noble gentlemen, with garments very threadbare, who make their daily appearance without any selfish object in view, but merely to see how it all goes off.

A quantity of pictures were lying about in disorder: with them were mingled furniture, and books with the cipher of the former owner, who never was moved by any laudable desire to glance into them. Chinese vases, marble slabs for tables, old and new furniture with curving lines, with griffins, sphinxes, and lions' paws, gilded and ungilded, chandeliers, sconces, all were heaped together in a perfect chaos of art.

The auction appeared to be at its height.

The surging throng was competing for a portrait which could not but arrest the attention of all who possessed any knowledge of art. The skilled hand of an artist was plainly visible in it. The portrait, which had apparently been several times restored and renovated, represented the dark features of an Asiatic in flowing garments, and with a strange and remarkable expression of countenance; but what struck the buyers more than anything else was the peculiar liveliness of the eyes. The more they were looked at, the more did they seem to penetrate into the gazer's heart. This peculiarity, this strange illusion achieved by the artist, attracted the attention of nearly all. Many who had been bidding gradually withdrew, for the price offered had risen to an incredible sum. There remained only two well-known aristocrats, amateurs of painting, who were unwilling to forego such an acquisition. They grew warm, and would probably have run the bidding up to an impossible sum, had not one of the onlookers suddenly exclaimed, "Permit me to interrupt your competition for a while: I, perhaps, more than any other, have a right to this portrait."

These words at once drew the attention of all to him. He was a tall man of thirty-five, with long black curls. His pleasant face, full of a certain bright nonchalance, indicated a mind free from all wearisome, worldly excitement; his garments had no pretence to fashion: all about him indicated the artist. He was, in fact, B. the painter, a man personally well known to many of those present.

"However strange my words may seem to you," he continued, perceiving that the general attention was directed to him, "if you will listen to a short story, you may possibly see that I was right in uttering them. Everything assures me that this is the portrait which I am looking for."

A natural curiosity illuminated the faces of nearly all present; and even the auctioneer paused as he was opening his mouth, and with hammer uplifted in the air, prepared to listen. At the beginning of the story, many glanced involuntarily towards the portrait; but later on, all bent their attention solely on the narrator, as his tale grew gradually more absorbing.

"You know that portion of the city which is called Kolomna," he began. "There everything is unlike anything else in St. Petersburg. Retired officials remove thither to live; widows; people not very well off, who have acquaintances in the senate, and therefore condemn themselves to this for nearly the whole of their lives; and, in short, that whole list of people who can be described by the words ash-coloured—people whose garments, faces, hair, eyes, have a sort of ashy surface, like a day when there is in the sky neither cloud nor sun. Among them may be retired actors, retired titular councillors, retired sons of Mars, with ruined eyes and swollen lips.

"Life in Kolomna is terribly dull: rarely does a carriage appear, except, perhaps, one containing an actor, which disturbs the universal stillness by its rumble, noise, and jingling. You can get lodgings for five rubles a month, coffee in the morning included. Widows with pensions are the most aristocratic families there; they conduct themselves well, sweep their rooms often, chatter with their friends about the dearness of beef and cabbage, and frequently have a young daughter, a taciturn, quiet, sometimes pretty creature; an ugly dog, and wall-clocks which strike in a melancholy fashion. Then come the actors whose salaries do not permit them to desert Kolomna, an independent folk, living, like all artists, for pleasure. They sit in their dressing-gowns, cleaning their pistols, gluing together all sorts of things out of cardboard, playing draughts and cards with any friend who chances to drop in, and so pass away the morning, doing pretty nearly the same in the evening, with the addition of punch now and then. After these great people and aristocracy of Kolomna, come the rank and file. It is as difficult to put a name to them as to remember the multitude of insects which breed in stale vinegar. There are old women who get drunk, who make a living by incomprehensible means, like ants, dragging old clothes and rags from the Kalinkin Bridge to the old clothes-mart, in order to sell them for fifteen kopeks—in short, the very dregs of mankind, whose conditions no beneficent, political economist has devised any means of ameliorating.

"I have mentioned them in order to point out how often such people find themselves under the necessity of seeking immediate temporary assistance and having recourse to borrowing. Hence there settles among them a peculiar race of money-lenders who lend small sums on security at an enormous percentage. Among these usurers was a certain . . . but I must not omit to mention that the occurrence which I have undertaken to relate occurred the last century, in the reign of our late Empress Catherine the Second. So, among the usurers, at that epoch, was a certain person—an extraordinary being in every respect, who had settled in that quarter of the city long before. He went about in flowing Asiatic garb; his dark complexion indicated a Southern origin, but to what particular nation he belonged, India, Greece, or Persia, no one could say with certainty. Of tall, almost colossal stature, with dark, thin, ardent face, heavy overhanging brows, and an indescribably strange colour in his large eyes of unwonted fire, he differed sharply and strongly from all the ash-coloured denizens of the capital.

"His very dwelling was unlike the other little wooden houses. It was of stone, in the style of those formerly much affected by Genoese merchants, with irregular windows of various sizes, secured with iron shutters and bars. This usurer differed from other usurers also in that he could furnish any required sum, from that desired by the poor old beggar-woman to that demanded by the extravagant grandee of the court. The most gorgeous equipages often halted in front of his house, and from their windows sometimes peeped forth the head of an elegant high-born lady. Rumour, as usual, reported that his iron coffers were full of untold gold, treasures, diamonds, and all sorts of pledges, but that, nevertheless, he was not the slave of that avarice which is characteristic of other usurers. He lent money willingly, and on very favourable terms of payment apparently, but, by some curious method of reckoning, made them mount to an incredible percentage. So said rumour, at any rate. But what was strangest of all was the peculiar fate of those who received money from him: they all ended their lives in some unhappy way. Whether this was simply the popular superstition, or the result of reports circulated with an object, is not known. But several instances which happened within a brief space of time before the eyes of every one were vivid and striking.

"Among the aristocracy of that day, one who speedily drew attention to himself was a young man of one of the best families who had made a figure in his early years in court circles, a warm admirer of everything true and noble, zealous in his love for art, and giving promise of becoming a Maecenas. He was soon deservedly distinguished by the Empress, who conferred upon him an important post, fully proportioned to his deserts—a post in which he could accomplish much for science and the general welfare. The youthful dignitary surrounded himself with artists, poets, and learned men. He wished to give work to all, to encourage all. He undertook, at his own expense, a number of useful publications; gave numerous orders to artists; offered prizes for the encouragement of different arts; spent a great deal of money, and finally ruined himself. But, full of noble impulses, he did not wish to relinquish his work, sought to raise a loan, and finally betook himself to the well-known usurer. Having borrowed a considerable sum from him, the man in a short time changed completely. He became a persecutor and oppressor of budding talent and intellect. He saw the bad side in everything produced, and every word he uttered was false.

"Then, unfortunately, came the French Revolution. This furnished him with an excuse for every kind of suspicion. He began to discover a revolutionary tendency in everything; to concoct terrible and unjust accusations, which made scores of people unhappy. Of course, such conduct could not fail in time to reach the throne. The kind-hearted Empress was shocked; and, full of the noble spirit which adorns crowned heads, she uttered words still engraven on many hearts. The Empress remarked that not under a monarchical government were high and noble impulses persecuted; not there were the creations of intellect, poetry, and art contemned and oppressed. On the other hand, monarchs alone were their protectors. Shakespeare and Moliere flourished under their magnanimous protection, while Dante could not find a corner in his republican birthplace. She said that true geniuses arise at the epoch of brilliancy and power in emperors and empires, but not in the time of monstrous political apparitions and republican terrorism, which, up to that time, had never given to the world a single poet; that poet-artists should be marked out for favour, since peace and divine quiet alone compose their minds, not excitement and tumult; that learned men, poets, and all producers of art are the pearls and diamonds in the imperial crown: by them is the epoch of the great ruler adorned, and from them it receives yet greater brilliancy.

"As the Empress uttered these words she was divinely beautiful for the moment, and I remember old men who could not speak of the occurrence without tears. All were interested in the affair. It must be remarked, to the honour of our national pride, that in the Russian's heart there always beats a fine feeling that he must adopt the part of the persecuted. The dignitary who had betrayed his trust was punished in an exemplary manner and degraded from his post. But he read a more dreadful punishment in the faces of his fellow-countrymen: universal scorn. It is impossible to describe what he suffered, and he died in a terrible attack of raving madness.

"Another striking example also occurred. Among the beautiful women in which our northern capital assuredly is not poor, one decidedly surpassed the rest. Her loveliness was a combination of our Northern charms with those of the South, a gem such as rarely makes its appearance on earth. My father said that he had never beheld anything like it in the whole course of his life. Everything seemed to be united in her, wealth, intellect, and wit. She had throngs of admirers, the most distinguished of them being Prince R., the most noble-minded of all young men, the finest in face, and an ideal of romance in his magnanimous and knightly sentiments. Prince R. was passionately in love, and was requited by a like ardent passion.

"But the match seemed unequal to the parents. The prince's family estates had not been in his possession for a long time, his family was out of favour, and the sad state of his affairs was well known to all. Of a sudden the prince quitted the capital, as if for the purpose of arranging his affairs, and after a short interval reappeared, surrounded with luxury and splendour. Brilliant balls and parties made him known at court. The lady's father began to relent, and the wedding took place. Whence this change in circumstances, this unheard-of-wealth, came, no one could fully explain; but it was whispered that he had entered into a compact with the mysterious usurer, and had borrowed money of him. However that may have been, the wedding was a source of interest to the whole city, and the bride and bridegroom were objects of general envy. Every one knew of their warm and faithful love, the long persecution they had had to endure from every quarter, the great personal worth of both. Ardent women at once sketched out the heavenly bliss which the young couple would enjoy. But it turned out very differently. "In the course of a year a frightful change came over the husband. His character, up to that time so noble, became poisoned with jealous suspicions, irritability, and inexhaustible caprices. He became a tyrant to his wife, a thing which no one could have foreseen, and indulged in the most inhuman deeds, and even in blows. In a year's time no one would have recognised the woman who, such a little while before, had dazzled and drawn about her throngs of submissive adorers. Finally, no longer able to endure her lot, she proposed a divorce. Her husband flew into a rage at the very suggestion. In the first outburst of passion, he chased her about the room with a knife, and would doubtless have murdered her then and there, if they had not seized him and prevented him. In a fit of madness and despair he turned the knife against himself, and ended his life amid the most horrible sufferings.

"Besides these two instances which occurred before the eyes of all the world, stories circulated of many more among the lower classes, nearly all of which had tragic endings. Here an honest sober man became a drunkard; there a shopkeeper's clerk robbed his master; again, a driver who had conducted himself properly for a number of years cut his passenger's throat for a groschen. It was impossible that such occurrences, related, not without embellishments, should not inspire a sort of involuntary horror amongst the sedate inhabitants of Kolomna. No one entertained any doubt as to the presence of an evil power in the usurer. They said that he imposed conditions which made the hair rise on one's head, and which the miserable wretch never afterward dared reveal to any other being; that his money possessed a strange power of attraction; that it grew hot of itself, and that it bore strange marks. And it is worthy of remark, that all the colony of Kolomna, all these poor old women, small officials, petty artists, and insignificant people whom we have just recapitulated, agreed that it was better to endure anything, and to suffer the extreme of misery, rather than to have recourse to the terrible usurer. Old women were even found dying of hunger, who preferred to kill their bodies rather than lose their soul. Those who met him in the street experienced an involuntary sense of fear. Pedestrians took care to turn aside from his path, and gazed long after his tall, receding figure. In his face alone there was sufficient that was uncommon to cause any one to ascribe to him a supernatural nature. The strong features, so deeply chiselled; the glowing bronze of his complexion; the incredible thickness of his brows; the intolerable, terrible eyes — everything seemed to indicate that the passions of other men were pale compared to those raging within him. My father stopped short every time he met him, and could not refrain each time from saying, 'A devil, a perfect devil!' But I must introduce you as speedily as possible to my father, the chief character of this story.

"My father was a remarkable man in many respects. He was an artist of rare ability, a self-taught artist, without teachers or schools, principles and rules, carried away only by the thirst for perfection, and treading a path indicated by his own instincts, for reasons unknown, perchance, even to himself. Through some lofty and secret instinct he perceived the presence of a soul in every object. And this secret instinct and personal conviction turned his brush to Christian subjects, grand and lofty to the last degree. His was a strong character: he was an honourable, upright, even rough man, covered with a sort of hard rind without, not entirely lacking in pride, and given to expressing himself both sharply and scornfully about people. He worked for very small results; that is to say, for just enough to support his family and obtain the materials he needed; he never, under any circumstances, refused to aid any one, or to lend a helping hand to a poor artist; and he believed with the simple, reverent faith of his ancestors. At length, by his unintermitting labour and perseverance in the path he had marked out for himself, he began to win the approbation of those who honoured his self-taught talent. They gave him constant orders for churches, and he never lacked employment.

"One of his paintings possessed a strong interest for him. I no longer recollect the exact subject: I only know that he needed to represent the Spirit of Darkness in it. He pondered long what form to give him: he wished to concentrate in his face all that weighs down and oppresses a man. In the midst of his meditations there suddenly occurred to his mind the image of the mysterious usurer; and he thought involuntarily, 'That's how I ought to paint the Devil!' Imagine his amazement when one day, as he was at work in his studio, he heard a knock at the door, and directly after there entered that same terrible usurer.

"'You are an artist?' he said to my father abruptly.

"'I am,' answered my father in surprise, waiting for what should come next.

"'Good! Paint my portrait. I may possibly die soon. I have no children; but I do not wish to die completely, I wish to live. Can you paint a portrait that shall appear as though it were alive?'

"My father reflected, 'What could be better! he offers himself for the Devil in my picture.' He promised. They agreed upon a time and price; and the next day my father took palette and brushes and went to the usurer's house. The lofty court-yard, dogs, iron doors and locks, arched windows, coffers, draped with strange covers, and, last of all, the remarkable owner himself, seated motionless before him, all produced a strange impression on him. The windows seemed intentionally so encumbered below that they admitted the light only from the top. 'Devil take him, how well his face is lighted!' he said to himself, and began to paint assiduously, as though afraid that the favourable light would disappear. 'What power!' he repeated to himself. 'If I only accomplish half a likeness of him, as he is now, it will surpass all my other works: he will simply start from the canvas if I am only partly true to nature. What remarkable features!' He redoubled his energy; and began himself to notice how some of his sitter's traits were making their appearance on the canvas.

"But the more closely he approached resemblance, the more conscious he became of an aggressive, uneasy feeling which he could not explain to himself. Notwithstanding this, he set himself to copy with literal accuracy every trait and expression. First of all, however, he busied himself with the eyes. There was so much force in those eyes, that it seemed impossible to reproduce them exactly as they were in nature. But he resolved, at any price, to seek in them the most minute characteristics and shades, to penetrate their secret. As soon, however, as he approached them in resemblance, and began to redouble his exertions, there sprang up in his mind such a terrible feeling of repulsion, of inexplicable expression, that he was forced to lay aside his brush for a while and begin anew. At last he could bear it no longer: he felt as if these eyes were piercing into his soul, and causing intolerable emotion. On the second and third days this grew still stronger. It became horrible to him. He threw down his brush, and declared abruptly that he could paint the stranger no longer. You should have seen how the terrible usurer changed countenance at these words. He threw himself at his feet, and besought him to finish the portrait, saying that his fate and his existence depended on it; that he had already caught his prominent features; that if he could reproduce them accurately, his life would be preserved in his portrait in a supernatural manner; that by that means he would not die completely; that it was necessary for him to continue to exist in the world.

"My father was frightened by these words: they seemed to him strange and terrible to such a degree, that he threw down his brushes and palette and rushed headlong from the room.

"The thought of it troubled him all day and all night; but the next morning he received the portrait from the usurer, by a woman who was the only creature in his service, and who announced that her master did not want the portrait, and would pay nothing for it, and had sent it back. On the evening of the same day he learned that the usurer was dead, and that preparations were in progress to bury him according to the rites of his religion. All this seemed to him inexplicably strange. But from that day a marked change showed itself in his character. He was possessed by a troubled, uneasy feeling, of which he was unable to explain the cause; and he soon committed a deed which no one could have expected of him. For some time the works of one of his pupils had been attracting the attention of a small circle of connoisseurs and amateurs. My father had perceived his talent, and manifested a particular liking for him in consequence. Suddenly the general interest in him and talk about him became unendurable to my father who grew envious of him. Finally, to complete his vexation, he learned that his pupil had been asked to paint a picture for a recently built and wealthy church. This enraged him. 'No, I will not permit that fledgling to triumph!' said he: 'it is early, friend, to think of consigning old men to the gutters. I still have powers, God be praised! We'll soon see which will put down the other.'

"And this straightforward, honourable man employed intrigues which he had hitherto abhorred. He finally contrived that there should be a competition for the picture which other artists were permitted to enter into. Then he shut himself up in his room, and grasped his brush with zeal. It seemed as if he were striving to summon all his strength up for this occasion. And, in fact, the result turned out to be one of his best works. No one doubted that he would bear off the palm. The pictures were placed on exhibition, and all the others seemed to his as night to day. But of a sudden, one of the members present, an ecclesiastical personage if I mistake not, made a remark which surprised every one. 'There is certainly much talent in this artist's picture,' said he, 'but no holiness in the faces: there is even, on the contrary, a demoniacal look in the eyes, as though some evil feeling had guided the artist's hand.' All looked, and could not but acknowledge the truth of these words. My father rushed forward to his picture, as though to verify for himself this offensive remark, and perceived with horror that he had bestowed the usurer's eyes upon nearly all the figures. They had such a diabolical gaze that he involuntarily shuddered. The picture was rejected; and he was forced to hear, to his indescribable vexation, that the palm was awarded to his pupil.

"It is impossible to describe the state of rage in which he returned home. He almost killed my mother, he drove the children away, broke his brushes and easels, tore down the usurer's portrait from the wall, demanded a knife, and ordered a fire to be built in the chimney, intending to cut it in pieces and burn it. A friend, an artist, caught him in the act as he entered the room—a jolly fellow, always satisfied with himself, inflated by unattainable wishes, doing daily anything that came to hand, and taking still more gaily to his dinner and little carouses.

"'What are you doing? What are you preparing to burn?' he asked, and stepped up to the portrait. 'Why, this is one of your very best works. It is the usurer who died a short time ago: yes, it is a most perfect likeness. You did not stop until you had got into his very eyes. Never did eyes look as these do now.'

"'Well, I'll see how they look in the fire!' said my father, making a movement to fling the portrait into the grate.

"'Stop, for Heaven's sake!' exclaimed his friend, restraining him: 'give it to me, rather, if it offends your eyes to such a degree.' My father resisted, but yielded at length; and the jolly fellow, well pleased with his acquisition, carried the portrait home with him.

"When he was gone, my father felt more calm. The burden seemed to have disappeared from his soul in company with the portrait. He was surprised himself at his evil feelings, his envy, and the evident change in his character. Reviewing his acts, he became sad at heart; and not without inward sorrow did he exclaim, 'No, it was God who punished me! my picture, in fact, was meant to ruin my brother-man. A devilish feeling of envy guided my brush, and that devilish feeling must have made itself visible in it.'

"He set out at once to seek his former pupil, embraced him warmly, begged his forgiveness, and endeavoured as far as possible to excuse his own fault. His labours continued as before; but his face was more frequently thoughtful. He prayed more, grew more taciturn, and expressed himself less sharply about people: even the rough exterior of his character was modified to some extent. But a certain occurrence soon disturbed him more than ever. He had seen nothing for a long time of the comrade who had begged the portrait of him. He had already decided to hunt him up, when the latter suddenly made his appearance in his room. After a few words and questions on both sides, he said, 'Well, brother, it was not without cause that you wished to burn that portrait. Devil take it, there's something horrible about it! I don't believe in sorcerers; but, begging your pardon, there's an unclean spirit in it.'

"'How so?' asked my father.

"'Well, from the very moment I hung it up in my room I felt such depression—just as if I wanted to murder some one. I never knew in my life what sleeplessness was; but I suffered not from sleeplessness alone, but from such dreams!—I cannot tell whether they were dreams, or what; it was as if a demon were strangling one: and the old man appeared to me in my sleep. In short, I can't describe my state of mind. I had a sensation of fear, as if expecting something unpleasant. I felt as if I could not speak a cheerful or sincere word to any one: it was just as if a spy were sitting over me. But from the very hour that I gave that portrait to my nephew, who asked for it, I felt as if a stone had been rolled from my shoulders, and became cheerful, as you see me now. Well, brother, you painted the very Devil!'

"During this recital my father listened with unswerving attention, and finally inquired, 'And your nephew now has the portrait?'

"'My nephew, indeed! he could not stand it!' said the jolly fellow: 'do you know, the soul of that usurer has migrated into it; he jumps out of the frame, walks about the room; and what my nephew tells of him is simply incomprehensible. I should take him for a lunatic, if I had not undergone a part of it myself. He sold it to some collector of pictures; and he could not stand it either, and got rid of it to some one else.'

"This story produced a deep impression on my father. He grew seriously pensive, fell into hypochondria, and finally became fully convinced that his brush had served as a tool of the Devil; and that a portion of the usurer's vitality had actually passed into the portrait, and was now troubling people, inspiring diabolical excitement, beguiling painters from the true path, producing the fearful torments of envy, and so forth. Three catastrophes which occurred afterwards, three sudden deaths of wife, daughter, and infant son, he regarded as a divine punishment on him, and firmly resolved to withdraw from the world.

"As soon as I was nine years old, he placed me in an academy of painting, and, paying all his debts, retired to a lonely cloister, where he soon afterwards took the vows. There he amazed every one by the strictness of his life, and his untiring observance of all the monastic rules. The prior of the monastery, hearing of his skill in painting, ordered him to paint the principal picture in the church. But the humble brother said plainly that he was unworthy to touch a brush, that his was contaminated, that with toil and great sacrifice must he first purify his spirit in order to render himself fit to undertake such a task. He increased the rigours of monastic life for himself as much as possible. At last, even they became insufficient, and he retired, with the approval of the prior, into the desert, in order to be quite alone. There he constructed himself a cell from branches of trees, ate only uncooked roots, dragged about a stone from place to place, stood in one spot with his hands lifted to heaven, from the rising until the going down of the sun, reciting prayers without cessation. In this manner did he for several years exhaust his body, invigorating it, at the same time, with the strength of fervent prayer.

"At length, one day he returned to the cloister, and said firmly to the prior, 'Now I am ready. If God wills, I will finish my task.' The subject he selected was the Birth of Christ. A whole year he sat over it, without leaving his cell, barely sustaining himself with coarse food, and praying incessantly. At the end of the year the picture was ready. It was a really wonderful work. Neither prior nor brethren knew much about painting; but all were struck with the marvellous holiness of the figures. The expression of reverent humility and gentleness in the face of the Holy Mother, as she bent over the Child; the deep intelligence in the eyes of the Holy Child, as though he saw something afar; the triumphant silence of the Magi, amazed by the Divine Miracle, as they bowed at his feet: and finally, the indescribable peace which emanated from the whole picture—all this was presented with such strength and beauty, that the impression it made was magical. All the brethren threw themselves on their knees before it; and the prior, deeply affected, exclaimed, 'No, it is impossible for any artist, with the assistance only of earthly art, to produce such a picture: a holy, divine power has guided thy brush, and the blessing of Heaven rested upon thy labour!'

"By that time I had completed my education at the academy, received the gold medal, and with it the joyful hope of a journey to Italy—the fairest dream of a twenty-year-old artist. It only remained for me to take leave of my father, from whom I had been separated for twelve years. I confess that even his image had long faded from my memory. I had heard somewhat of his grim saintliness, and rather expected to meet a hermit of rough exterior, a stranger to everything in the world, except his cell and his prayers, worn out, tried up, by eternal fasting and penance. But how great was my surprise when a handsome old man stood before me! No traces of exhaustion were visible on his countenance: it beamed with the light of a heavenly joy. His beard, white as snow, and his thin, almost transparent hair of the same silvery hue, fell picturesquely upon his breast, and upon the folds of his black gown, even to the rope with which his poor monastic garb was girded. But most surprising to me of all was to hear from his mouth such words and thoughts about art as, I confess, I long shall bear in mind, and I sincerely wish that all my comrades would do the same.

"'I expected you, my son,' he said, when I approached for his blessing. 'The path awaits you in which your life is henceforth to flow. Your path is pure—desert it not. You have talent: talent is the most priceless of God's gifts—destroy it not. Search out, subject all things to your brush; but in all see that you find the hidden soul, and most of all, strive to attain to the grand secret of creation. Blessed is the elect one who masters that! There is for him no mean object in nature. In lowly themes the artist creator is as great as in great ones: in the despicable there is nothing for him to despise, for it passes through the purifying fire of his mind. An intimation of God's heavenly paradise is contained for the artist in art, and by that alone is it higher than all else. But by as much as triumphant rest is grander than every earthly emotion, by so much is the lofty creation of art higher than everything else on earth. Sacrifice everything to it, and love it with passion—not with the passion breathing with earthly desire, but a peaceful, heavenly passion. It cannot plant discord in the spirit, but ascends, like a resounding prayer, eternally to God. But there are moments, dark moments—' He paused, and I observed that his bright face darkened, as though some cloud crossed it for a moment. 'There is one incident of my life,' he said.

'Up to this moment, I cannot understand what that terrible being was of whom I painted a likeness. It was certainly some diabolical apparition. I know that the world denies the existence of the Devil, and therefore I will not speak of him. I will only say that I painted him with repugnance: I felt no liking for my work, even at the time. I tried to force myself, and, stifling every emotion in a hard-hearted way, to be true to nature. I have been informed that this portrait is passing from hand to hand, and sowing unpleasant impressions, inspiring artists with feelings of envy, of dark hatred towards their brethren, with malicious thirst for persecution and oppression. May the Almighty preserve you from such passions! There is nothing more terrible.'

"He blessed and embraced me. Never in my life was I so grandly moved. Reverently, rather than with the feeling of a son, I leaned upon his breast, and kissed his scattered silver locks.

"Tears shone in his eyes. 'Fulfil my one request, my son,' said he, at the moment of parting. 'You may chance to see the portrait I have mentioned somewhere. You will know it at once by the strange eyes, and their peculiar expression. Destroy it at any cost.'

"Judge for yourselves whether I could refuse to promise, with an oath, to fulfil this request. In the space of fifteen years I had never succeeded in meeting with anything which in any way corresponded to the description given me by my father, until now, all of a sudden, at an auction—"

The artist did not finish his sentence, but turned his eyes to the wall in order to glance once more at the portrait. The entire throng of auditors made the same movement, seeking the wonderful portrait with their eyes. But, to their extreme amazement, it was no longer on the wall. An indistinct murmur and exclamation ran through the crowd, and then was heard distinctly the word, "stolen." Some one had succeeded in carrying it off, taking advantage of the fact that the attention of the spectators was distracted by the story. And those present long remained in a state of surprise, not knowing whether they had really seen those remarkable eyes, or whether it was simply a dream which had floated for an instant before their eyesight, strained with long gazing at old pictures.

Lightning Source UK Ltd.
Milton Keynes UK
UKOW051853241111

182637UK00001B/214/P